The Religious
and
Other
Fictions

Book design by Lindsey Quinn Arroyo
and Neal Ranjan Shyam
Cover design by Grinning Moon Creative
Images from the Mix N Match Virgin Mary set are
reproduced with permission from Blue Q, Pittsfield,
MA.
Library of Congress Control Number: 2005933840
ISBN-13: 978-0-88748-453-7
ISBN-10: 0-88748-453-0
Copyright 2006
Printed and bound
in the United States of America

The Religious

and
Other
Fictions

Christina Milletti

Carnegie Mellon University Press
Pittsburgh 2006

Seeme they religious?
Why so didst thou.

—SHAKESPEARE

TO:

Paul West,
Don Byrd,
Pierre Joris,
Dave Kress,
Christine Hume,
Edward Desautels

— and my family —

my special thanks

For Dimitri

CONTENTS

Retrofit

I.

"You're real Mexicans now!"

Chencho-Mac laughed as he pulled over to the side of the road and toward a young couple, a young American couple he quickly surmised (knowing by sight, as any good cabby would, the Yank from the Frenchman, or the Anglo from the Slav) who, with their luggage strapped on their backs, were walking away from San Miguel toward the northern stretch of the island. The walk from the pier wasn't far, but they hadn't counted on the rain. Like most Yucatán storms, it had loosed in a panic from the clouds above and, quite simply, they were drenched. More than drenched, they looked exhausted. *Who wouldn't be exhausted playing the part of a burro?* he thought, waving to them as he stepped from his convertible VW Bug and, as though kindly, offering them each an umbrella before telling them his fare for a ride. It was hiked, of course, but they agreed without question. They climbed in even as Chencho-Mac explained that he always drove with the Bug's top down—that the top stayed down even in the worst of weather—because the vinyl had shrunk in the Mexican sun and would no longer snap in place. Wiping the rain from their chins, his new clients shrugged. It was no weather to bargain in and so, huddling close, they set the umbrellas over their heads like helmets, then draped the damp blanket Chencho-Mac hid under the seat over their legs to keep them warm.

At heart, Chencho-Mac was an honest man. He never cheated. Had never stolen. Above all (he often told his wife): he never told a lie he did not first believe himself—this being just one of the many lectures he thumped eloquent before his meals, the others involving the bullfight (though he himself had never attended), and, of course, the allure of the American woman, whose hair always smelled of aged liquor as though this is what she washed it in and, dried on the stem, what set it in place. To all of this, his wife would snort and turn back to the stove. If she were in a feisty mood though, she might mutter loudly, "You're just a Chencho-liar." Her reply, as rote as his lectures, reminded him, though there was no need, that she had learned to translate *him* as much as his words—such as his sudden desire for orthodontic devices, for the braces he'd bought just the day before. He claimed he got them at cost.

"The Americans," he explained before he'd gone to the dentist, "they only trust a man if he can smile a *bona fide* smile like their own."

"They are of course quite stupid," she remarked without thinking, not expecting him to stomp his slight frame across the kitchen, trying hard to go heavy so his steps would resonate through the shack's thin walls. He only succeeded in rumpling, in some cases, tearing up the newspaper he'd laid for her like tiles on the floor. She smoothed them out after he left, added new sheets to patch up the holes, and when he came home three hours later, he showed off his grin and the wires that framed it. He kept rubbing each tooth. Poking at the swollen gums to make them bleed.

"You're a crow," she said as she peered into his mouth. "Hiding jewels in that maw of yours."

Mouth open, he simply grunted as she sprayed water and lime juice over each tooth to cool off the gums and heal them more quickly. Then he winced, dipped a finger in the cup and rubbed the juice on his teeth himself.

"You'll see," he said. "These will pay off nicely."

She nodded absently, then gave him a cosmetic mirror which Chencho-Mac used to examine his braces, wiping, with the hem of his shirt, the fug of his breath from the mirror's face before shoving the mirror in his mouth again and, eyes somewhat crossed, staring down at his nose, trying to see if his smile had begun to pull more broadly, if his teeth had moved the fraction the orthodontist had promised by the end of the month.

That night before they fell asleep Chencho-Mac pulled at his wife's thigh and, happy, squeezed the flesh of her hip in his palm.

"I see a difference already," he told her.

"Yes," she said. "You now have a Chencho-shrine."

Sighing, she rolled toward the side of the bed farthest from him.

The next day, all trace of the heavy rain had evaporated in the sun by the time Chencho-Mac arrived at the docks to meet the first incoming ferry. He parked, he smiled, he stood up in

his seat "like a Jack in a Bug," he told the couple approaching—
warily—which he liked. More Americans. He liked Americans,
he told them. The blond, though skinny, wasn't bone thin like
some of the young girls who came to San Miguel and pretended
to be women. Her friend, he was wiry and confident, and it
was with the confident man that Chencho-Mac played his best
games, taking advantage of the over-plumed ego and his own
good nature.

They had a hotel? Why yes, they told him, though they
were staying for only two days. Just two? Why so few? Because
they needed to get home—where it was snowing! said Chencho,
to which they all chuckled. Yes, where they lived, it was cold all
right. Imagine, the young fellow said, five feet of snow and ten
foot drifts if you were in the right spot. The woman coughed:
Our home is in the right spot. They were married, Chencho-
Mac spied the rings. They weren't newly-weds though; they no
longer worried their rings as most newly-weds did, like half-
formed thoughts. He'd bet they'd been married for at least a
year, but not less.

"Well I will tell you," he said slowly, letting the sweat from
his lip collect on a knuckle before wiping it on his shirt. "This
island, as you know, is the largest in all Mexico. You'll need a
car to get around, to the other side, to the north, the south, and
into town for the night. The center, it's all jungle, nothing there
but diving bugs." Chencho-Mac leaned toward them as though
confidentially: "Now, I will take you to your hotel. You take
a shower, make yourself at home in your rooms, unpack. And
then at noon, I'll come back for you and show you around, your
own private tour, to the best beaches, the best shops, or if you

want the quiet place, you tell me and I'll take you there too. Best yet," he said when they began to shift uncomfortably, "I have no fee. At the end of the day, when I take you home at dusk or dawn, you and your pretty wife together think it over: then you pay me what you think is right." He waved them toward a small alcove in the stone wall that ran along the docks. "You go and talk it over, I won't be offended." He bowed slightly and closed his eyes. They waited for him to open them, as had so many others, then turned and walked a few steps away.

Chencho-Mac slipped out of the Bug and, as he would many times more in the days to come, began to shine the car with a soft cloth he stowed under his seat, buffing the paint slowly to give his clients the portrait of accustomed nonchalance they'd come to Mexico to see. In a few moments they returned. They were sold.

Chencho-Mac grinned the wide-open grin the infidel shares with the infant, and loaded their bags under the hood as the woman leaned on the passenger door. "My name is Alice," she said, introducing herself as she counted each bag with her eyes. Chencho-Mac smiled, he had a fine smile. "And my daughter," he said, "her name is Alicia!" He pointed to a picture of his neighbor's daughter which he'd pinned to the glove compartment. "Just five years old and already she counts the change her papa brings home at night." "How bright! You're very lucky," said Alice who liked children—especially children in pictures—then she stepped back to admire the Bug.

"I didn't know Volkswagen made these any more," she told him. "I used to have one in college."

Chencho-Mac smiled. "Maybe later I let you drive."

And then they were off to the Cozumel Club. Alice was a teacher, she told Chencho. And John, he was a dentist. John had just opened his first practice, bought it off a fellow who, whirring drill in hand, had a heart attack and, in the midst of his seizure, grabbed hold of the rinsing fountain, electrocuting himself before the patient, mouth stuffed with cotton, could knock him to the ground. Strangely, though, the fellow survived because the charge put his heart back to rights.

"My god," said Chencho-Mac. "Two days ago, I went to the dentist. To the orthodontist." Chencho bared his teeth in the rearview mirror, weaving through two rental cars driven by tourists and a bus driving unusually slow. "Look," he said, waving for John to sit up in his seat and look in the mirror, not toward the road and a truck filled with milk crates on which they were bearing too fast.

"Look!" Chencho-Mac said again, and cut sharply around the truck.

John looked. "Braces."

"Braces!" said Chencho-Mac, smiling as they caught up to another taxi which abruptly took a right onto a small, unused road. In the back seat of the car—a shiny convertible Bug much like his own and one he recognized as belonging to Papa José, the young man the ladies called Papa because he'd had so many girls—sat a woman who looked like Chencho-Mac's wife balancing a frying pan on her knees, pushing the long dark hair blowing around her face with one hand from her eyes.

"One moment," Chencho-Mac said, as he pulled the car to the side of the road, choked the Bug's gears, and ran over a sign fallen to the pavement long ago when a tourist knocked it over.

Chencho-Mac quickly explained to the Americans that he had passed a turnoff to an attraction of such a subtle nature that he often didn't show it to the tourists he escorted around the island. Alice and John, however, were different. They must know how unlike they were from the tourists with whom they arrived on the ferry; being refined Americans, they no doubt could bridge the unpredictable discourse between a Mexican and his neighbor.

"There is something I'd like to show you," he said.

Making a U-turn at the next break in the median, Chencho-Mac returned to the small sand trap of a road down which Papa José had driven his taxi, setting the Bug's wheels in the taxi driver's tracks to avoid the shifting sand that threatened to stall the convertible. Fifty feet down the road, the uncut jungle blocked their view to the sides and, as though down a chute, Chencho-Mac rolled the car and its occupants slowly, commenting quickly on the various insects stunning themselves on the windshield, on the sounds of the geckoes chirping, on the seabirds cruising in line over others rustling the mangroves. His clients were content as he carried on; after all, they were on a tour of the Mexican jungle which, they surely had read in their guidebooks, was home to the jaguar and manatee, to the crocodile and wild boar, forgetting, because of the denseness of the brush and the small fierce trees, that they were no longer on the mainland, that the chief predators of the island jungle were stray tomcats and large birds—as well as mosquitoes, of course, which they'd begun to swat at briskly.

Around a bend, the road came to a halt. Confused,

Chencho-Mac put the Bug in neutral and considered the duplicity of Papa José and the cleverness of his wife. Evidently, they had seen him and had quickly broken off their rendezvous. Even now, Papa José would be dropping off Chencho-Mac's wife and the frying pan she brought with her. They certainly weren't hiding; the jungle was impassable, the brush, far too thick for such a light car, even a durable one as the Bug, to roll into and hide.

No one, Chencho-Mac thought, is here.

II.

When the knock came that evening, it was not on the front door which was not a front door but a curtain. Nor was it knocked on the door-frame which framed the curtain and to which Chencho-Mac's wife pinned the dark fabric to keep it from blowing open much as someone might lock a door. Instead, her husband rapped his knuckles against the window sill looking into the kitchen where Chencho-Mac's wife stood over the stove rotating the frying pan with quick sure movements above the burner's blue flame, banging the pan down sharply when it became too heavy for her wrist to bear. From the pan came the scent of garlic, of cilantro and lime masking the sweet sting of chile. She was cooking up a feast.

"Chencho-Mac," she acknowledged without turning around. "Your supper is almost ready."

He nodded. Though she did not see him nod, she imagined it, each of his nods being more like a tic, a jerking of the skin by the corner of his mouth, which gave the illusion that he had tossed his chin much as a stubborn horse will seem to shake its head at a pest when it has only blinked its eye. A moment later, she heard him wrestling with the pin and the curtain, and then refastening the curtain against the frame as he stepped inside their home. Chencho-Mac sat down at the kitchen table as his wife brought over a stew of conch and squid with a basket of tortillas.

"You've cooked a feast," he said.

"A strange thing happened today, Chencho-Mac," she said as she set down his plate. "I have a story to tell. Will you listen while you eat?" He nodded and so she began.

"Today after you left in the morning, I did, as I always do, the wash and the dishes, I fed the chickens and your father's mules, I pitched the barn and watered the garden, planted some chiles. At noon I came in to rest and make myself some hot chocolate. I was standing at the stove when the knock came much like yours this evening, a knock rapped not on the door but on the sill of the window looking into the kitchen where I was standing melting the chocolate. It was not you of course. I knew it was a stranger by the way he rapped his knuckles: firm so I would hear the knock over the sound of the pot pinging from the burner and the boiling milk. But the knock was yielding too, so I wouldn't be angered by the intrusion, as though I would be flustered by a neighbor's arrival if the neighbor didn't call first.

"'My name is Schnee,' he said, and so I invited him in. How could I not invite him in after I began to stare at him like the town children stare at tourists? You know how the children act. How they run by the tourists, dodge them just to get close, to smell them, to touch their clothing, pick pockets like some of the older ones do. And there I was acting just like them, staring at this man—Schnee he said his name was—and so I took him to be German, though not just because of the name: he also held himself as Germans do, as if his shoulders were linked by bone to his hips. There he was, then, not in the square but at my house, nearly in my kitchen, at least part of him, the hands on the sill, the head and neck leaning in. I would not have it: Chencho-Mac, I have my pride.

"'My name is Schnee,' he said again as though I had not heard the first time, and so, because I wanted to study him but not stare at him, I invited him into our home.

"Now this man, he was not handsome, or tall, nor was he overly strong. Quite simply, his head was far too large for his body, which was not so small itself, the head just oversized for the average broadness of his shoulders and his neck to bear. The man was a hopeless carnival, one of the traveling kind with fine equipment gone shoddy, not with age, but lack of care. This Schnee, he wore his linen pants like that—with the hems let down—and his shirt, it was clean but of a pattern long since passed in fashion. And though he walked with his head held high—I can only imagine the effort—his head wobbled, shimmered really, a sound ship tossed on a gross rebelling sea, up and down it went as we sat together. My god, it was a sight.

"Would you believe he was a salesman? A scout sent to evaluate the Mexican market for retrofitting light fixtures? He was a light bulb salesman, Chencho-Mac, selling a long life, energy efficient light bulb that costs as much as three regular ones, but lasts as long as six.

"'Would you, Señora Mac, be interested in such a

product?'

"He asked this somewhat coyly, and, if he'd had a hat, I think he would have tipped it then. As it was, he did something queer with his fingers, as though on their way past his nose and up toward the hat that was not there, he realized he'd forgotten it, so each finger cramped as he dropped his hand to his side.

"At any rate, that's when I told him we only have one lamp, and suggested, to be helpful, that he'd be better off inquiring at the hotels on the coast whose managers worry about such expenses far more than we do.

"And then, this Schnee, he looked around the room, at the loveseat and the rocker and the little stand with our one lamp, and nodding—he was so polite this German with the great big head—he rose from where he sat, said 'Thank you for your time' as most salesmen do, and quietly passed through the curtain."

"He went next door, to Papa José's house?"

Chencho-Mac's wife shook her head. "No. He simply walked down the road as though he'd been to all the other homes already. But when I asked the neighbors if the German had paid a visit, none of them had seen him."

"Perhaps he picks homes randomly?" Chencho-Mac suggested.

His wife shrugged. "Who's to say? I watched him to the corner. The hem of his pants dragged up the sand in the street and it must have got into his shoes because, before rounding the corner, he took them off, tucked both shoes under one arm, and, barefoot, walked back toward town. For a man with such a large head, he moved quickly, because no one on that street saw him either. I am, it seems, the only one."

For Chencho-Mac, there remained the matter of confirming his wife's story, which is to say, he wondered, could not sleep for wondering—which was rare for him and so, he thought, unhealthy—when to trust one's wife and not one's eyes. There was also the question of proof: his was the glimpse, his wife's, the tale: which was he to trust?

So Chencho-Mac went to see his friend, the fisherman, Gordo. He brought along his clients, Alice and John from the day before. At the front of the fish store he dropped them off, leaving them with Gordo's son, Pepe, who began to show off the morning catch in the buckets around the counter—the fresh squid marinating in its own ink, shrimp and clawless lobsters. Meanwhile, Chencho-Mac found Gordo in the back room, smoking a cigarillo and reading the morning paper. Chencho-Mac joined him as he often did and, sweeping the table free of the ash which always collected on it, he leaned in on his elbows, retelling his wife's story, though not the reason why.

"Have you seen such a man?" he asked his friend. "I myself would have liked to. My wife, she said it was something, to have this strange man in our house, to have his great big head bobbing outside the kitchen. This island is not so big that a man with such a large head can easily hide. I would like to find him."

Gordo shrugged. "But how large is large my friend? Like a cut from the cheese wheel? Like a ball? Like the bosom of Papa

José's latest girl?" He chuckled. "Perhaps his head was not so large. Perhaps this German's neck was simply small. Perhaps it is your wife who is lacking a sense of proportion."

"Are you suggesting my wife made up this story?" Chencho-Mac pulled over a section of the newspaper and began to study its headlines while Gordo carefully formed his words so as not to insult his friend.

"Now Chencho-Mac," he began, "the lie usually comes in the plain package, no? A quick trip to the market, for instance, when the feet in fact intend to take the liar somewhere else. Now this story—your wife, she would have to be foolish to make up such a tale. I merely suggest that she perhaps sees things not as they really are."

"And how are they really?" his friend wondered.

Gordo laughed. "You are Chencho-Mac. Things are as you see them."

At the front of the store Alice and John were debating whether to buy squid or lobster. But their hotel room, they realized, did not have a kitchenette.

"We'll cook it here for you," Pepe explained, "and tonight, for dinner, you pick it up. Chencho-Mac will bring you."

"I have a better idea," Chencho-Mac interrupted, as he and Gordo emerged from the back room. "Tonight, you will eat at my house. My wife, she has only one skillet, but she uses it exceedingly well. It is, of course, why I married her."

Pepe nodded. "It's true."

Chencho-Mac stepped back and bowed. "I would be honored to have you visit my home for the evening, unless, of course, you have other plans."

"No plans," Alice said after her husband nodded. "We'd love to come. At what time should we expect you?"

"Why wait?" said Chencho-Mac. "Let's go now, have an early supper, and then I will take you to the best place for dancing. Is this not your last night in San Miguel?"

III.

By the time the knock came that afternoon, Chencho-Mac's wife had pulled off her apron and rinsed her mouth with lime juice, she had already wiped her face of sweat and oil and pushed the loose strands of her long dark hair back behind her ears.

"Chencho-Mac," she acknowledged without turning around. "Who have you brought with you?"

"The Americans."

"Tell me," she said simply.

"You will cook them dinner. There is a cooler from Gordo under the hood of the Bug. We will pin the curtain and the shades. We will light candles by the loveseat where they will sit and eat their meal."

She paused and turned. "You've never brought tourists before to our home."

"Until yesterday, a German never stood in the kitchen."

After a moment she nodded, and Chencho-Mac stepped back through the curtain. By the time he returned with their guests, there were several glasses of water set out on the table arranged around a small bowl of lemons.

Alice paused as she took in the kitchen. "We haven't put you out I hope?"

"Of course not," Chencho-Mac's wife said in her direct way. "We enjoy having guests."

"And as you know," the cabby bowed, "I like Americans."

Alice smiled. "And we like you." She raised her glass. "We like your stories."

Chencho-Mac's wife began slicing a lemon. "My husband," she said, "always tells stories well."

"As does my wife," he added.

"And your daughter?" John asked.

Chencho-Mac's wife turned to her husband. "Our daughter?"

"She's at school," said the cabby.

John frowned. "On Saturday?"

The cabby sighed. "It's because of the strikes."

"That's nice for the parents."

Chencho-Mac's wife smiled softly. "Oh, she's never a chore."

"And so bright says your husband."

"I'm not surprised," Chencho-Mac's wife said as she began warming tortillas. "He's always been proud of his family."

"You must be tired," Chencho-Mac said to his guests an

hour later—after he had given them a tour of the barn, showed them his mules and the garden, the chiles his wife grew there, the serrano and poblano, the jalapeño, the habañero. "Of course you're tired," he said when Alice and then John protested. "Now come inside!" Chencho-Mac pulled John by the elbow and his wife by her arm. "Here you will take your first real siesta, here in my home. You honor me." Through the small living room, they followed him, giving in quickly because they were in fact tired, drained by the heat of the afternoon sun. In his cool, dark bedroom, Chencho-Mac gave them a sheet and a knit blanket too; they soon would feel chilled without the sun on their skin. He shook out their pillows, then helped them take off their shoes.

"I will come to wake you," Chencho-Mac assured them, "when the meal is ready." He shut the door behind him softly and went to find his wife.

She was leaning on the kitchen sill, looking out beyond the Bug and toward the tracks the car had made in the sand, her gaze fixed, it seemed, on the places where Chencho-Mac's footsteps obscured the car's tracks, tossed up the sand unevenly so that the seabirds came down hunting for crabs, crosshatching the sand once again with their new and hasty prints. She might have been thinking, he thought, about the nature of time, how to mark its passing when the events that seem to imprint it, obscure even older markers, unsettling them and so displacing the very ones she relied on. She might have been thinking, in short, that Chencho-Mac—as a man of action—no doubt had a plan, a scheme, because there always was a scheme. Certainly, she was wondering why he had brought the Americans, why he had invited tourists into her home and made of it a stage.

She did not turn when he entered, acknowledging him by ignoring him as she often did: she turned her back so that he would know that she knew he was there.

"A strange thing happened today," he said, sitting down at the kitchen table. "My wife," he said, "I have a story to tell you. Will you listen while you cook?" She nodded and, turning slowly to face him, returned to the pan sitting cool on the stove. With a match, she lit the pilot and watched the metal begin to flex against the heat.

"When I left this morning," he began, "I drove, as I always do, directly to the Pemex station where I filled the Bug's tank and washed the tires, checked the oil and swept the back seat free of sand. I bought a cola and a chocolate and, though I ate the chocolate right there at the station, I saved the soda for later. I hid the bottle under my seat because you never know where you'll get stranded when there are Americans about. By ten, I was off to the hotel where my clients are staying, and though we had made an appointment for noon, I went over early to talk business with Old Pinto, the hotel's concierge. I was on my way, driving not too fast since I had room enough in the back to give someone a ride when, to my surprise, I spied a fellow who looked like the German you described last night, the light bulb salesman with the great big head, sitting by the road, his knees pressed up into his chest as if he'd been folded like a box. In his hands, he held a light bulb. Without thinking, I pulled over. I wanted to ask him about the product he had walked so far to sell the night before.

"'It is the light bulb you're selling?' I asked. He was lethargic, unaware, it seemed, of my presence and of the nearby car, of the dust I'd kicked up as I'd approached. He didn't answer and so I sat down by him, waiting because there is always time—too much of it—and finally he responded as if he had not made me wait.

"'One needs the fixture for the light, and, here, there are few fixtures. That is what I wrote.'

"'What you wrote?' I asked.

"'In my report.' A moment later: 'Is it better to be fired sooner or later?'

"'Why wait?' I counseled because, as you know, I am a man of action, but my answer only made him sigh and, pulling his knees to his chest even tighter—I can only imagine the effort— he balanced the bulb on his knees.

"'Since dawn,' he said slowly, 'I've been thinking on this question, whether to go, whether to stay. If the moving makes a difference.' He paused and looked me over as though I might know the answer. 'You are clearly a man of action.'

"'Of course,' I said because it was true.

"'That is a gift,' he said. 'It is a gift to know something. To *know* it, you understand, beyond all the doubts that are among the knowing.'

"He fell silent then, and uncertain what to say, I merely watched him contemplate the light bulb on his knee. He was silent for a long while, but I was in no rush—Old Pinto would remain where he was, at the hotel where he has always worked, smiling at guests who would continue to come, borrowing favors and hopefully giving some business to me.

"Finally, the German spoke up.

"'I see you have a car,' he said, his chin jerking toward the

Bug, his eyes lingering on it before resting again on me. 'I will make you a deal,' he said. 'I will loan you this light bulb now if, in one hour, you return to see if I'm here.' During that hour, he explained, he intended to contemplate his future, if he had such a thing, and if his future were bright, what he should expect from it: which is to say, if one should in fact hope for a bright future at all, this sounding to him, he said, far too luminous and in need of retrofitting.

"He laughed half-heartedly at his joke, and I joined him: I had never met a German who did not get straight to the point.

"Schnee paused for a moment. Then, like an old door, he began to move, shaking out one arm and extending the light bulb toward me.

"'How long have you had this light bulb?' I asked him.

"He may have winced then. Perhaps it was a smile.

"'My friend,' he said simply, 'recollections are all that we have, memories not like pictures, but like little myths. They gain strength over time as we retell them. In time, one need never tell them again.' He gazed longingly at his light bulb then and, under the force of his gaze, I slipped it into my pocket. I tucked it away like an idea whose moment hasn't yet come to pass.

"'I have not always been a failure,' he added before I drove away. I must admit, I believed him because he spoke the words without inflection as though he'd never had to convince anyone of it before.

"I returned as promised an hour later, but without the light bulb he gave me in good faith and which I gave to Old Pinto in the same way—to seal a business arrangement. Yet even before I helped the German into the back of the Bug, he asked for it, as if it were the light bulb's return and not the ride to the ferry that he'd been looking forward to while I was gone.

"'I'm afraid,' I explained when he asked for it back, 'there was an accident.'

Schnee said nothing for a moment, though it seemed to me that his neck was suddenly thinner, that under the weight of his massive skull, his neck curved and his shoulders bent. I've never seen a grown man look so uncomplicated and sad.

"'It is wise perhaps,' he finally said, 'to every so often lose a thing one holds dear in just such a fashion.' He sighed then and quite suddenly I felt sad too. Though I couldn't say why.

"'Let me make it up to you,' I told him. 'Why not join my wife and I for dinner tonight?'

"The German thought this over for a moment, and then agreed. 'I am, after all, quite hungry.'

"'Excellent,' I said. And in fact, I was pleased, far more curious about the salesman, his light bulbs, not to mention, his large head, than I had imagined. So I drove him into town and dropped him at the plaza. Before he left, though, he promised to come for an early supper tonight. In fact, he's late," Chencho-Mac said, looking at his watch. "He should have been here by now."

"More guests?" said Chencho-Mac's wife.

"Indeed," her husband replied. "It's a regular dinner party."

By the time Alice and John woke from their nap, the

table was set, the candles were lit. Chencho-Mac had stuffed extra pillows beneath the loveseat's cushions to make their guests' seat more comfortable. There was water in the glasses, and, at the table's center, an ashtray filled with scented straw. Chencho-Mac had washed his face, his wife had changed her dress. The warm scent of fish and lemon was hanging in the air and everyone was hungry.

When Alice and John emerged, Chencho-Mac guided them to the loveseat and, sitting them down, pulled over the table and tucked its edge beneath their ribs. He then gave John a bottle of wine, explaining, as the American unscrewed the cap, that, though their meal was ready, they were still waiting for a tardy guest. He was a German, Chencho-Mac said, a very unusual German, a salesman, but more than a salesman, an average-sized man with a great big head out of scale with the rest of his body. His name was Schnee, and to this Schnee, he was indebted for reasons he'd rather not say, since the salesman was not only a private man, but a modest one as well.

"He's a salesman you say?" Alice asked.

"Of light bulbs," Chencho-Mac said. "A long life energy efficient light bulb that costs as much as three regular ones but lasts as long as six."

"Ah," said John. "He's a retrofitter."

His wife nodded. "Germans often retrofit."

"Do you know many Germans?" Chencho-Mac asked.

Alice took a sip of her wine. "Who doesn't know Germans?"

"I know Germans," John said. "In fact, many of my

patients are Germans, if not German, which is to say, from Germany, than certainly of German origin, their parents or grandparents having been German and having brought their culture with them. I can always tell a German by the way he shows me his teeth."

"Do they all have such large heads?"

"They certainly have large teeth," said John, pouring himself another glass of wine. Then he smiled and tapped his rumbling belly. "Perhaps when your German arrives, we can take up the matter with him."

There is always the question of hunger, which is to say, how hungry one may be at any given moment, how much food one requires to alleviate the abject sensation of a belly empty but for air. Such questions must be ignored, however, when one is a guest, as Alice and John were guests (even tourists) of their cabby's home. They of course had read at length about Mexico and its people—how hospitable they were, how friendly, how they always doted on the guests they invited to their homes. Though, as the Americans sat an hour later staring at their hands around the empty table, they could not help but think that their guidebooks had been wrong or, at the very least, left out essential points—idle thoughts made worse because the Americans were drunk. How could we not be drunk, Alice thought, with so much wine, so little food, with the smell of squid and garlic hanging damply in the air. Chencho-Mac's wife looked around. Her guests were hungry, it was clear to see, toying with their knives and forks, as they considered, she imagined, the nature of food and time, above all, the punctuality of Germans. This is no way, she thought, to start a dinner party.

"I'm sorry for the delay," Chencho-Mac said. "I'm sure Schnee will be here soon, let's wait a few more minutes."

"It's the least we can do," Alice said politely.

"Yes," John added. "The least."

When a half hour had passed and, still, Chencho-Mac would not allow his wife to put the meal on the table, Alice finally pressed him: "Are you *sure* Schnee is coming?"

"You understand," he told the Americans, "our rules of hospitality."

"Of course," Alice said quickly while John smiled, as though good-naturedly, through the candle's flame and toward their hosts. Chencho-Mac returned the gesture, his lips pressed and curling as he looked at each of them in turn, last of all at his wife, who glanced away when his eyes fell slowly on her.

A while later, John was finishing a story about a patient who, after taking pain medication John had prescribed, became convinced he was a dentist himself. "Can you imagine?" John said. "And when his wife had him call me—she was worried, you can see why—he thought *I* was *his* patient. Needless to say," he went on, "the fellow was fine once he stopped taking the stuff. Afterwards, though, he enrolled in my alma mater: I hear he graduates a dentist next month." John began pounding his fists on the table, teeth bared as if he were laughing, though he made no sound. Alice tried to grab his arm but, overshooting the mark, instead missed and spilled a glass of water. Chencho-Mac's wife rose and brought her a dry towel.

"How much longer must we wait?" Chencho-Mac's wife whispered to her husband.

"As long as it takes," he whispered back.

"And how long will it take?"

"How long is the walk?"

"The walk is not long."

"Then the wait will be short."

"But the wait has been long," she snorted.

"Then Schnee must walk slow."

"But I've seen him walk fast."

"No doubt, it's perplexing."

"Which means something's wrong."

"Which means," her husband corrected, "he'll be hungry when he finally arrives."

Fifteen minutes later, Alice sent a pleading look across to their hostess who abruptly stood up.

"Come with me," Chencho-Mac's wife said to her husband, pointing to the kitchen. He followed her and found her standing at the stove, back turned to him as she tapped the frying pan on the burner. "This cannot go on," she said as he pulled the curtain after him to block their guests' view. "Chencho-Mac, what are you and the German scheming?"

"I have no scheme, wife."

"You still think Schnee's coming?"

"Guests often are late."

She grunted. "Last night, Schnee told me that a good salesman's never late. That a salesman who wants to make a sale must be on time and that, because a salesman always likes to sell, he always *is* on time."

"Schnee said that?" Chencho-Mac frowned. "He told me that, though a salesman always likes to sell, a salesman sometimes should be late: that selling is in the timing."

"Much like a meal!" she added, banging the pan.

"But what of Schnee?"

"Schnee is not coming!"

"How do you know?" her husband asked almost gleefully.

They paused an unkind pause, stepping back from one another as John rustled, then pushed through the curtain into the kitchen. He studied his hosts' flushed faces. "I don't mean to interrupt," he said flatly, "but I thought you should know that your German just stopped by." Unsteadily, he leaned against the kitchen wall. "What I mean is that your Schnee just stopped by. But then he left. He claimed he was in a great, big hurry."

Wordlessly, Chencho-Mac and his wife studied each other. Then after a moment, they followed John back to the table.

"I didn't believe it, you know," John said as they began to eat the tepid meal, the squid ceviche which had shrunk, as meals often do, when they've been overcooked. "Frankly, a German with such a large head was hard to imagine. But your salesman, this Schnee we waited for this evening, my—what a fellow—I've never seen anyone like him. He was..."he paused, searching for words.

"He was mammoth," Alice said.

"Mammoth," John nodded. "Yes that's it. We'd never seen anyone like him."

"Now I must admit," John went on, "your Schnee was in a rush, he couldn't stay long, he said, not even long enough to apologize to you personally for holding up our meal."

"He was rude," Alice said.

"No," John corrected, "not rude, in a rush. Alice and I were talking softly when we first heard the knock. The knock was soft at first. At first I didn't hear it. It's not so late, but late enough: your German must have thought you'd gone to bed. At any rate, I got up, I knew it was him. Who else were you expecting? I was right of course, and there he was when I pushed the curtain aside, there he was, your German, the retrofitter you'd described. How quiet he was. Too quiet for such a large man bearing an enormous weight on his neck. Then again, he just might have been thinking about what to say, because when he at last spoke, his message seemed rehearsed."

"Like lines someone's practiced," Alice said.

"Exactly," said John. "He had poise, I'll give him that—wordless but with his poise—standing just outside the door. After a moment, he stepped inside and let the curtain fall behind him. He looked around, at the table all set up, at the wine, the empty plates, at the rocker where Chencho-Mac is sitting, finally at the lamp."

"'How kind of you to wait for me,' he said at last, 'But I must leave at once. I'm late you see, I'm going home. You'll witness for me won't you? You'll pass on my apologies? You'll tell our hosts I'm sorry, that it's unavoidable that I must go?'

He paused and studied us, nodding his thanks as though we'd agreed. 'We all must go home eventually,' he added. 'And I'm tired of translating.' He stepped close to me and held out his hand. 'As Americans,' he said as I gave him my own, 'you must know what I mean.'

"He didn't wait for me to answer, and, to tell the truth, I wouldn't have known what to say. But then he nodded and, shrugging, said simply, though with apparent effort, 'Thank you for your time.' Just like that! 'Thank you for your time,' as most salesmen do, and that was all he said. Then he turned and walked out the door, pulling the curtain after him, and it was as though he'd never stopped by at all. It wasn't until I heard his steps fading, in fact, that I realized how final his words seemed. You know how salesmen are when they thank you for your time, how they say it meanly because it's not what they intend. But your Schnee, he wasn't at all like that. How serious he was, melancholic even. In his words was something final, I'd bet on it, as though the time he spent with you was over, a finished thing, as though he stopped by to take back his time, to take it with him on the ferry, to rescind it and take his time back with him all the way home."

John paused and then looked at his hosts.

"I suspect you won't see him again."

IV.

The next morning, Chencho-Mac found Gordo in his office at the fish market. As usual, the fisherman's feet were on the table, a paper on his knees; in his fingers, the cigarillo he always smoked while reading; on the table, the soot he left behind. Chencho-Mac sat down and swept the table free of ash, pulling toward him a section of the paper Gordo had cast aside.

"Did you find the man you were looking for?" Gordo asked, folding the pages neatly before he offered the cabby his full attention. Gordo would finish reading the news after Chencho-Mac left; he always finished the paper before giving it to his friend when he returned in the evening to pick up meals Pepe cooked for the tourists.

"My friend," Chencho-Mac said slowly. "I have a story to tell you. Will you listen while you smoke?" Gordo nodded and so the cabby began.

"Last night, as you know, I invited the Americans into my home, I asked them to meet my wife, and sample her cooking. Even the German, that salesman I told you about, was going to come. I wanted to study him, but not stare at him, to share some stories perhaps over a glass of wine.

"But when Schnee at last arrived—my friend, there is no other man like him—I stepped back from the door, I stepped aside, I moved out of his way to give him more room. It was his head just as my wife explained. The head—like a fat squash on a doll—as if a sleepy seamstress had sewn the two together as she was nodding off. There he stood: an average sized man with a great big head, held high less by strength than by pride. His hands, they were empty however. The light bulb was gone: he must have sold it after all.

"Now the German, he didn't stay long, he just dropped by to pay his respects. In fact, after drinking just one glass of wine, he left us, tipping a hat that was not there and saying, as most salesmen do, 'Thank you for your time,' that was all, nothing else. Even the Americans noticed how final his words were, how formal he seemed when he left. Schnee didn't just thank us, you see, he thanked us for our *time*, as though that time was now *his* time and he was taking it with him in exchange for the light bulb. There it was between us—the time we shared—and as Schnee collected it up like loose sand in a jar, I knew he'd take good care of it. So I relinquished it to him. As did my wife. Even the Americans who, you'd think, wouldn't have known any better.

"We gave him our time. And he took it. It's his gift, I think, this taking of time. So we gave it to the German with the great big head and he took our time to keep."

Chencho-Mac fell silent as Gordo continued to smoke, blowing smoke rings which grew and enclosed them, then dissolved.

"Soon your Schnee will be legend," Gordo said at last, shaking his head slowly.

Chencho-Mac shrugged. "Legends are always made of such men."

Gordo thought on this a moment, then laughed a soundless laugh as he crushed his cigarillo beneath his foot. "My friend," he said, cutting the smoke with his hands, "did you think legends are ever made from men such as us?"

The Smallest Apartment

In the smallest apartment, 1000 girls lived in a single room
and slept on a single orange couch. Their lips parted, they
dreamt as one. As one they awoke, swung 2000 slippered feet
onto the floor. Then they sidestepped—that's all it took—into
the smallest kitchen. There, 1000 girls ate from a single bowl
with a single spoon. They didn't shower. What bathroom, their
long dead mother once said, was big enough for 1000 girls?
Then she laughed (1000 girls still remembered her laugh) and,
gently slapping their 1000 bottoms, she turned—one could only
turn in the smallest apartment—and washed their single dish.

After breakfast, 1000 girls sidestepped back to the couch
and, passing a basin and cloth from one girl to the next, they
soaped their skin and rinsed their hair. Pink and damp, their wet
hair in ringlets against the back of their necks, 1000 girls then
turned on the smallest t.v. set in the smallest apartment where
they'd always lived. They watched the black and white picture
until, their limbs hung out like wash on a line, 1000 newly dry
girls fell asleep.

1000 girls lived in harmony. They'd always lived in harmony. Until one day it was discovered by chance that 12 of the girls were boys.

988 girls stood up and shook their fists, they stomped their feet. Then they opened the door—it opened only a crack before it thumped the back of the couch—and pushed the 12 impostors into the hall.

That night while they slept, several girls fell off the couch without the bracing bodies of their neighbors. Still others had nightmares for the first time in their lives. The vacant space in the smallest apartment made them uneasy they said: where once there were sighs, there was only dead air where 12 boys used to sleep. Evidently, the smallest apartment was far too big. What, they thought, should we do?

That next evening, and every evening thereafter for one week, 988 girls slept fitfully; they tossed and turned as 1000 girls never had. 12 boys, meanwhile, did not return. They did not knock on the door or beg for reentry. Once out in the hall, they simply had stumbled away.

To complicate matters, the girls couldn't eat. In the mornings when they turned to the kitchen, each girl now offered to hold their single spoon. 988 girls didn't know what to do. So they put the bowl away.

988 girls realized they needed advice.

We've changed, they told a therapist from the edge of their seat. Once we were 1000. Now we are less.

Do you feel like less? the therapist said.

We *are* less, 988 girls answered as one. Because we're no longer more. What, they sighed, should we do?

The therapist paused and, for one moment, 988 girls swelled with hope.

He leaned forward. Do you think that's the right question to ask?

988 girls returned to the smallest apartment and sat together on the couch. Having wrapped every arm around every belly, 988 girls tried to feel calm.

Several hours later, a note arrived for them under their door. It slipped through the crack, under the couch, then behind the smallest t.v. set in the smallest apartment where 988 girls bent to retrieve it.

Come outside, 12 boys had written in the uneven script of 12 right hands. *Meet us at the café this evening. We have something to show you.*

988 girls opened the apartment door just a crack (a crack of course was all it would open). But, as one, 12 boys had disappeared down the hall. They were already gone. Back into the street.

That evening, 988 girls met 12 boys as 12 boys requested. Together, 1000 sat in a plush red booth. Together, they ordered 2 coffees. They'd never ordered 2 coffees before.

We have lived, 12 boys said, in the smallest apartment since we were born. 1000 children in the smallest apartment with one couch, one bowl, one spoon to share. One television to watch from the orange couch for almost nineteen years.

12 boys squinted at 988 girls. Do you like living in the smallest apartment?

988 girls sipped one coffee and tapped their feet. They pushed the sugar they'd spilled with just one spoon around the red checkered cloth on the table.

We have always lived in the smallest apartment, they said. The smallest apartment is where we were born.

12 boys rose and took 988 hands. Together, if not as one, 1000 left the booth and crossed the street. Then they walked to the building next door. Together, they rode the elevator. Together, they walked down a carpeted hall and stepped into a vacant apartment.

Inside, a thin man with a beard waited by a large, bay window. He hiked up his pants as 1000 walked in. Then he looked at his watch.

You're late, the superintendent said. Without another word, he led them through the apartment—from the eat-in kitchen, past the large, claw foot bath. Around a corner, a fireplace, through several bedrooms.

As you can see, he said, there is plenty of room for a family here. 1000 can live with ease.

988 girls considered the space.
It won't be the same, they finally said.
12 boys nodded as one boy. Yes, they said, it will be different.

As one, 988 girls turned and left. Once again inside the smallest apartment, they shut the door, sat on the couch. Huddled together, they found there was even more space in the smallest apartment than there had been that same morning.

Carefully, 988 girls turned around the apartment. 1976

eyes quietly examined their home.

In the smallest apartment, there was a sink, a drain. A small vent to daylight. It was big enough for the orange couch, even the smallest t.v. set propped on its smallest stand. Their basin and cloth were within easy reach. As was their bowl. And their single spoon.

As one, 988 girls flexed 9880 toes.
The smallest apartment was perfect.

Where Nööne
Is Now

There is a sequel to this story. It has already been written: no doubt my sister Nööne has already corrected my mistakes. After all, this is her story. I'm merely telling half. The half I know. Which is to say: I know nothing at all. Nööne has said as much for years.

Even now, after all that has happened, I can imagine Nööne ringing my bell on Avenue J, returning to the house in which we grew up, and those would be her first words. Without greeting. After three years. *Don't make assumptions, you know nothing at all.* Why shouldn't she say it? In the past, she's always been right.

It is just like Nööne to always be right.

After she left for China, Nööne kept in touch with my mother (I missed her phone calls). Then—suddenly—we heard nothing from her. Not a word. Not a letter after the Chinese embassy in Belgrade was bombed. Not even an e-mail since my sister went into hiding. Even when my mother fell ill and died.

That's another story. A story only half related to this one which is (as I've said) only in part mine. This story is my sister's story as she told it to my mother who then told it to me sixteen days after NATO bombed Belgrade and my mother saw, while propped in her bed, an international news report about a young American woman who was beaten as she walked through the

Beijing streets on her way to work. The young woman, my mother said, looked like Nööne. She had fended the blows as Nööne might fend them, she had even fallen as Nööne often fell. My mother wasn't wearing her glasses when she saw the report. She was under heavy medication, morphine in fact, in the last stage—the only stage—of the rapid illness that took her. So I reassured her, I stroked her damp face: *Leave it alone. Don't worry,* I said. I no doubt smiled at her distress: *You know Nööne always lands on her feet.*

Let me be clear: I did not smile because I care little for Nööne, even though we have never been close, or even troubled by the fierce rivalries that generally mark complex sibling relations. The fault is mine, I have no doubt: I'm not sentimental. I did not weep as my mother did, for instance, when Nööne moved to Beijing three years ago to pursue graduate studies. Yet I felt uneasy as Nööne's airplane rose off the tarmac from Newark Airport: it has always been impressed on me—I'm not sure by whom—that you ought to keep your family close. Perhaps that's because Nööne and I have different fathers. Because I am the elder and, unlike Nööne, I have never known mine.

So when I smiled at my mother, I did so merely to comfort her as one might comfort a child who awakes bewildered in a strange bed in the night. I smiled because her fears were groundless, because—as she herself had known—Nööne hadn't lived in Beijing for over a year. Not long after Nööne earned a Masters degree in Eastern Political Studies from Northern JiaoTong University, she'd left the city. But while her peers had gone on to consult for big business or statesmen,

Nööne had just moved from Beijing to Yuxian—a nearby village in Hebei Province where the rice paddies are especially dry. There, she collected data and wrote reports for *China Today,* a Chinese magazine published in English by an expatriate staff based a world away in New York. At first, Nööne only worked freelance. But three months after her first piece appeared, *China Today* brought Nööne on board full time. As usual, I was happy for her. I was happy because my mother was happy each time *China Today* arrived in the mail, as if it were a letter addressed only to her: *CT,* after all, was the closest my mother came to a dialogue with my sister—came to an understanding of where Nööne was and why—during the years she was away. Her phone calls were too short, my mother complained. Nööne never told her enough about where she lived, what she ate, the few friends that came to visit. So it was no surprise that my mother forgot about Yuxian: there was so little for her to hang onto once she became ill. She forgot Nööne's move as easily as she forgot the small curved wound on her back that long ago had scabbed up, then scarred, after she accidentally tripped over my sister on Avenue J. At the time, Nööne was two. I was ten. So it was I who dutifully applied the ointment to my mother's back.

As my mother lay damply against the fresh sheets of her bed, I didn't remind her that Nööne had moved from Beijing. I didn't tell her because I would have then also had to remind her where Nööne lived *now*—why she'd left Yuxian. I would have had to relate the events that transpired after Nööne took her degree. And I didn't want to make her remember how fiercely she worried, her prolonged distress, when early one morning (one week to the day she was diagnosed with her illness) Nööne's advisor called from Yuxian in alarm. There was sweat in his voice. I could hear it bubble against the dry swell of his throat, though he tried to speak slowly—each accented word arriving soft and precise through optical cables laid across ocean floors. He took his time. He explained with sober attention how the police visited Nööne's home that evening. How two officers— two stern-faced men paired in green serge—had interrupted them shortly after he arrived for a visit, just as they sat down to share a kettle of tea. *They took Nööne's laptop,* he said. *Her notes. Articles under revision. Even drafts of letters she was writing home.* A Ministry man then dragged her collected belongings outside while Nööne was escorted to a dark, idling car. They were gone in an instant. The advisor's tea was still warm as the car pulled away in the direction of Tiajin, where the cargo ships docked. There, Nööne was put aboard ship the next morning. A colleague watched the engines catch, dredge yellow water as the ship pushed out to sea. Of Nööne, however, the advisor's colleague saw nothing. Yet my sister's fate was apparent to all: without explanation, the police had sent her away by ship. Nööne was expelled from China.

There was no news from her for three weeks as the freighter made its way south for Taipei, then west to Danang, before it pressed onward to Krong Kaoh Kong. It wasn't until the ship drew up along the sudden madness of Thailand's southern coast that the Captain, following the Ministry's orders, at last passed her off. *We are behind schedule,* he said as he secured a rope ladder, tossed it over the side, then gestured for her to climb down. No doubt Nööne left his crew without a word. That would be like her: to climb with care down the rope until her feet touched the new deck. To leave her captors without complaint.

The deaf fisherman who met her aboard his vessel didn't question the sudden, extra company, Nööne told my mother. He just handed her a gutting knife. Then showed her how to pin a squirming eel under her foot, while she thumped a rock on its head. They spent the afternoon together like that— leisurely gutting his catch while the freighter disappeared in the distance—before they at last made their way back to shore.

Nööne called at once to tell my mother what happened: she was safe at the docks at Laem Chabang. She had no money, she said, but she did have a job: an editorial post already lined up with *China Today* (a new branch, she said, had opened in Bangkok). She was lucky, Nööne was clear about that. Though the editor hadn't expected her, he was sending a car to pick her up at the docks. He'd even offered to put her up a few nights, at least until she found an apartment. *I'm unharmed*, she said, *there's no need to worry.* She would ring again soon when she had her own place. And she did: three weeks later she called (I was at work). She spoke to my mother, spelled the names of the streets my mother couldn't pronounce. I have since written Nööne. In fact, I wrote frequently when my mother first became ill. All my letters, however, have been returned. I am quite sure Nööne remains unaware that our mother has been dead now four months.

Yet I'm still not concerned. Nööne is like the wind—as proficient, as perilous. She can slip through doors. Beneath window sills. She can always get in and out when she desires. To this day, even her name remains a mystery to me. It can't be pronounced in my mother's tongue. Nor in Nööne's father's.

And in the English common to our home, it makes no sense at all. I say "Nuh-oon." My mother "Noh-woon." My sister uses both names and many others. When I was young, I used to ask my mother about it. But with a half-smile, she'd shrug, as though in her gesture lay an approximate answer—an enigma I know Nööne still enjoys. It was a game between them. And if they shared a secret, I didn't begrudge them or the distance between us: it was just how things were, how I knew they'd always be. We grew up as though nurtured in two different nests. Even if by the same, doting bird.

At the kitchen table, my mother sat nervously not long after the freighter first left China. She looked slightly blue, as if the belt she'd cinched up several notches were strangling her slowly like a lazy serpent. It was just an illusion. Under the fabric, I knew her belt was still loose. Already, my mother was losing weight (the treatments were taking their predicted effect). Already, we knew she was dying. I did what I could: I warmed up her tea, I held her hand. I offered small words of comfort.

You know Nööne, I said and kissed my mother's red knuckles. *She is like wind,* I went on, *as proficient...*

My mother slapped me then. A hard stinging blow. It took her some time to rise from the table, and slowly return to her bed.

Don't get me wrong. I do worry about Nööne, just not unnecessarily. After all, Nööne has left us hanging before (just not for so long). It's the nature of her assignments, of "collecting data," she'd say. Eight months is a protracted silence of course. Yet *China Today* is still sending her paychecks—that's what they tell me. And Nööne's stories continue to appear with comforting, albeit anonymous, frequency (for "security reasons," her editors claim). One piece per issue, that is, every two weeks. But for the first time out of Belgrade.

Nööne's move was a surprise of course: I thought she was still in Bangkok, much as my mother thought Nööne was still in Beijing. Yet Nööne had traveled suddenly, swiftly, before at the behest of her editors. And *China Today*, I reasoned, likely developed an interest in the Balkans when the Chinese embassy (as Nööne was quick to point out against contrary claims) was targeted by NATO and bombed. *Can the public believe, as they seem to believe, that the intelligence maps were merely "old?"* she wrote. *That our armed forces act no differently than city teens lost in a corn field at night?*

I have no doubt of course that Nööne is writing the series. Nor do I have trouble imagining how she must have prodded her editors for it, pushed them to send her, to allow her to be the first American writing from Belgrade for a Chinese paper published in New York. The geographic stitchwork of her position no doubt would have pleased her: it's just like my sister to position herself one step away from what she desires just to get exactly what it is that she wants. She's strategic that way. Ambitious. I once watched her leave a ballpark after a surly pitcher declined her interview. A moment later, she appeared at his side through a trapdoor in the mound. The pitcher relented in surprise of course. That's always been Nööne's way.

I once asked her about it. We are not close, but I've always wanted to understand my sister, her motives, better. Nööne merely looked at me from the sides of her eyes as though I'd asked a much different question. *If I am symbol*, she said, *I merely stand in for myself.* Then she met my gaze. *But only at certain frequencies.* At the time, she was working for a local news desk, it was her first job as a sports stringer during college. She was only a kid, they didn't give her an office—just a desk and a chair with a blind at her back. The chair creaked as she rocked. It had four casters, and one didn't spin. As we spoke, she rocked in her chair.

Two years later, Nööne left for China.

While in Kosovo, I gathered Nööne was the guest of a man she called Danilo Losvek (the name no doubt was a pseudonym), a professor of social history. The life of his family, my sister wrote, had been "disrupted by a conflict that was not their own." Danilo likely would have had a lot to say on the matter. But it was his daughter whom Nööne quoted at length. "Lena Losvek, 18, points up to the craggy apex of a mountain above her village" (I read). "'The rebels are there,' Lena explains. 'But they do not shoot. They do not want us to know what we already know: that they have received new weapons.' 'Who sent them?'" the reporter asks. Lena does not answer, but the reporter describes the look in her eyes, rich and brown, fresh earth pawed by a goat in a meadow. "'When the army shoots at them,' Lena says, 'they hit us instead.'" She sounds as grim as an eighteen year old youngster can sound who, until the year before, ate potatoes and chocolate, bought new clothes without question. "'They are lousy shots.' Lena kicks a small stone into the sewer. 'But even lousy shots are sometimes lucky.'"

Within 24 hours, the international news agencies—all of them—picked up Nööne's feature. By all accounts, the story should have made the back page. It was a focus piece—sentimental—not hard news, like most of her work. Yet in less than a day, after one year's work, Nööne's career was suddenly launched. Only I and *China Today* knew she was the source of the story, but I'm sure, somewhere—back in her hotel in Belgrade perhaps—Nööne must have been pleased. She likely smiled—the faint smile of those whose hard work has paid off—as she relaxed, feet up in her slippers, newspapers strewn on the floor.

What do you think of that? I asked my mother as I always had in the past. Had she been at home, and not in her grave, she would have cried *Bravo!* So I said it for her: *Bravo, Nööne, bravo!* Alone, I leaned on my mother's tombstone, against her freshly carved name, as if it could give me warmth.

Your sister has a way in this world, a way with *this world,* my mother would have said, *which most of us can't understand.* When she said "us," I knew my mother meant "you." That is, she meant "me": "they" had an understanding from which "I" was excluded. That much was apparent to me from an early age. Perhaps because my mother loved Nööne's father more than mine, even if both left her without warning. Mine in a rush hour pile up on the Garden State Parkway before I was born. Nööne's father, one morning, to go "west." It was a trip from which he never returned.

Where is Nööne? Where is she now? my mother asked me each morning when I arrived at the hospice to sit by her as she faded often mid-sentence in and out of consciousness, hemming in a thought over a course of hours—one word or phrase at a time—until she locked her punctuation in place with a tired and forced smile. *Where is Nööne? Where is she now?* That was the gist of it. I tried to answer her. That is, I lied. *She is in Hong Kong,* I'd say, *but the flights are grounded. She has landed in Tokyo, don't be afraid. Nööne called,* I told her, *but she's been diverted to Sydney.* Some days later, *Hawaii at last!* Then: *San Francisco (she's so close I can feel it).* Towards the end, it was *Reno* then *Houston. Detroit,* at last *Philly.* The geography was all wrong. The geography didn't matter. *Soon,* I assured my mother. *Soon.* I lied again and again. I mailed letters. I called *China Today.* Nööne was simply beyond reach. Long before my mother died, I gave up on her. My mother never did.

I buried my mother in the local cemetery, adjacent to the university football stadium where Nööne scooped her first story. I can still remember how proud my mother was of that first publication, how she carefully clipped it and pinned Nööne's work to the kitchen wall. Now matted and framed, the article still hangs where my mother once placed it. Though my mother herself is gone.

The story appeared to be simple at first. The state university had lost a "big game" they were favored to win, and after two overtime periods, several controversial calls, one fight, one fine, and a raging crowd, the game finally let out in disbelief. The town was afire with unwieldy fan passion, and Nööne and I were inside the crowd when a short, steamy riot broke out in the streets. Like a wave whose tide licks your calves before it tosses you onto your back, we felt the gentle nudge of its wet rumble begin. Nööne was first to notice of course. She grabbed my arm, held me back, as a young, painted woman (Jerzy Min was her name) turned and, winking at Nööne, picked up a trashcan not five steps from us. Without a sound—it happened so quickly—the heavy can was aloft in her arms. A moment later, she'd hurled it, clumsy but sure, through the thick glass of a barbershop window. The glass shattered and, pleasure being equal portion expectancy and satisfaction, Jerzy clapped her hands, crushed the scattered shards beneath her feet. Soon, she was jumping, the crowd was jumping. *Yes*, Jerzy shouted, fists beating the air. *Yes!* I knew what she meant: *Yes! That's much better.* It was as if I could hear her thinking it as she was carried off across the sweaty oxbow necks of the crowd, her palms to the sky, holding it up, as if her strength were its only support. *I am the world*, I thought I heard her sing. I shook my head while Nööne took notes.

Why do people destroy, I asked?

Nööne looked at me in surprise, the way she always has.

Why not?

I knew not to challenge what she meant, though she asked Jerzy the same question the next morning during a follow up interview. Jerzy's answer, "Because the world is destroying us," was remarkably prescient. Spoken at home in Cog Country,

USA, the center of Newark's industrial garden—not just after a football game, but, more significantly, we later learned, while an Apache helicopter with 9 airmen aboard was shot down overseas—it captured the tenor of a new global paradigm that was as apparent to high school dropouts as elected statesmen. Nööne's piece about Jerzy made the front page.

For any other novice reporter, their first story would have been innocuous. Words and ink quickly lost to fiche, to the archives of aging librarians. Yet Nööne was uncanny. I said she was the wind. But perhaps she's really a witch. I used to find her staring at the moon as if she understood what it meant to be large and alone, looming over the earth, giving off one's light to the blind.

Two years after that football game, Nööne left the country to pursue her graduate studies. After that, I never saw her again.

In the first few months after graduation from Northern JiaoTong University, Nööne was hired as a research analyst to gather agricultural data in Yuxian. She wasn't disappointed with the job, though we knew she missed being a reporter. *Data is just a story told on a spreadsheet*, she explained to my mother over the phone, *you just have to learn how to tell the facts right, learn how to read them.* Her job was to count people, births, the length of days. To note blisters, infections. To remark on the subtle bend of stiff spines beneath cotton, to estimate crop production, the average wage for each family. It wasn't long before the locals took to her, she said, offered up recipes to complete her records, even invited her into their homes for evening meals. Afterwards, she often stayed up to watch the stars align just to note how long her subjects slept and, if they slept, how deeply they dreamed. In the morning, she transcribed their visions. How, that night, Xu fished deep waters. Shao bought pink fabric. Or Zhu made the cracked town bell sing as it never sang for its maker, an arthritic blacksmith, 400 years before.

Once, I found a note Nööne had scrawled during an unexpected return trip home while I was away on business. My mother didn't tell me Nööne dropped in. I only learned about her brief visit after I found the note, and my mother confirmed that Nööne passed through before she went to New York to meet her editors for the first time in person. *Our chief trouble,* Nööne wrote, *is our belief in fact. A coin has 2 sides. A globe has many. They bend, overlap. A curve is nothing but a distortion.* Beneath this she had written in lowercase letters: *i have too much pride.*

When my mother died, I ordered her tombstone from a man who claimed he was my mother's countryman and, because of their erstwhile relation, gave me a 10% discount. *You know,* he told me as I wrote down my mother's name, her relevant dates, *you spell your surname wrong. It's not possible to say your name in our language. To say it the way it's spelled, understand? There are too many consonants. This way, your name sounds like a sheep skin stretched between posts.* He paused, crossed out two letters added three more. *You should correct it,* he says. *Your mother should be buried with her own name, not the name someone else gave her as a girl when she first stepped off the boat.*

I thought for a moment. My mother had never told me about the misspelling. Perhaps she never knew. She hadn't gone to school for long before her father sent her to live with her American cousin who fed me sweet rice when I was a child. After her cousin died when I was eight, however, it was just my mother and I, eventually Nööne. How were we to know of the error if my mother didn't herself?

Do it, I told the engraver, and with a curt nod, he made the correction. Later, I took the paper with her new, old name home, pinned it by the telephone next to Nööne's postcards. *It is never too late to be buried under another name,* I'd told the engraver. *We should all be corrected after we die.* The engraver had squinted at me. *I wouldn't have guessed,* he said, *that you inherited a sense of humor from the country of your mother's birth.* He laughed. *You speak her language much better than you know.*

At home, there was a message on my answering machine. At last, I thought, at last Nööne has heard, at last she has called. I wasn't surprised, however, that the voice wasn't hers, but that of the American consular representative in Beijing with whom I'd spoken two weeks before when I'd been promised a prompt reply. His message was brief. Nööne was still on file with the American Embassy in Beijing. But they had no record of her expulsion. Nor a new registry under her name in Bangkok. Was I aware, he asked, of her work with *China Today*? Was I aware that Northern JiaoTong University wasn't accredited back in the States? He asked: Was I *aware*?

I called the consular representative back. *I did not mention before,* I told him, *that my mother believed she saw Nööne during an international news report broadcasted from Beijing. My mother saw Nööne chased by a crowd, beaten by men in the streets.* I heard the consular representative grind his teeth. He was annoyed, enamel on porcelain. I heard it all though he hadn't spoken a word.

What news agency, he asked? I didn't know. He paused (he was thinking: was I *aware?*). *Call me back when you remember.*

My mother's skin smelled like dust before she died and I often considered collecting her, sweeping her up like talc into a bottle so I would be able to powder myself with her scent in the days to come.

Do you remember, she asked, smiling faintly as I pulled a thin blanket around her shoulders, *I tripped you up on the sidewalk? You fell, you were just two. I cried when I saw your blood.*

I still have the scar, I said pointing to my lower back. I was uncertain if she thought I was Nööne or if she'd forgotten, as she'd forgotten so much else, that it was Nööne who tripped her (not the other way around). But I didn't remind her. Instead, I held her hand until she fell deeply asleep. She was still smiling faintly as though the memory of tripping Nööne gave her great and unexpected pleasure.

The consular representative called me back the next day. *Evidently, we store video recordings of news broadcasted by the local networks for up to 3 months*, he said. *It will take time, but I will look through them for you.*

Can I help? I asked him. *Should I come to Beijing?* He paused. I could hear him chewing his tongue. *That would be a breach of security.* Since the tapes were already broadcasted, I couldn't see how. But I didn't argue. Instead, I quietly hung up the phone.

He called back one week later. Nööne had in fact been in Beijing, the representative told me. After the footage was originally aired, the embassy had looked into it, found Nööne, and interviewed her. The report was duly filed, my sister had signed it. He read the report to me over the phone.

"In Beijing," Nööne was quoted as saying, "not long after the Chinese embassy was bombed in Belgrade, I went to buy produce. I went to buy three bananas. Not many, just enough for the next few days. They turn brown too quickly in the summer heat, you must go buy produce every few days or the flies come and stick to your eyes while you're napping. I was at the market, at a fruit stand. I did not touch the bananas, you cannot touch them, you're not supposed to. You have to wait," she explained to her interviewer, "until the old woman emerges from behind the stand. Then you point out the fruit you want, and she bags them for you, that's how it's done, that's how I'd done it for years while I lived in Beijing. The old woman knew me, though I'd been gone one year. I was just back for a visit. As usual, I pointed at the bananas. They were green still, under ripe, but I was sure they would turn quickly. I bent, I pointed. And while my eyes were turned, while I was distracted, the old woman hit me. She slapped me hard, right here on the side of my head. She punched me with the small tough fists that once patted my back while I lived in Beijing. She screamed, the other patrons watched. I could not hit her. I dared not. You saw the tape. I wanted to, that's true enough," Nööne said. "If we'd been alone, I think I would have belted her. One good shot to the chin, that's all. I could have knocked her out. I could have left her there flat on her back. But it was a good thing I ran instead because the men showed up quickly. They kicked me once, maybe twice. But I run fast. I left them all behind."

She stopped then and for the first time asked a question herself.

"I was caught on camera? I was broadcasted on the evening news?"

The interviewer didn't record his response.

The consular representative cleared his throat. *That's the end of the file.*

Where is Nööne now? I asked.

There was a long pause. *I'm afraid,* he said simply but without comfort, *the interviewer failed to inquire about your sister's current residence. She gave only her former Beijing address. I have no idea why.*

He paused then. *Do you?*

I didn't bother to answer: of course I didn't. I know nothing at all. It's the only thing of which I've ever been sure.

Nööne's university advisor called today. *I thought I might help you,* he said. *I thought I could find an address, a lead perhaps. Instead, I've just discovered to my surprise that Nööne never registered for classes at NJTU. In fact, though she wrote a thesis, and I graded her work, she never took a degree. She was here for two years. Now she's gone. That's all I can say.* As an afterthought he added: *She was my favorite student.*

Since then I've learned there's no bell in Yuxian. There isn't a town hall from which Nööne sent her stories. There is no Shao, no Zhu. There is no China. Only desolate monkeys eating jicama aloft in the trees.

You are an accumulation of the events of your life, Nööne once told me. *What you have done is not who you are, but who you become. Always stay on the move.*

Not long after, I received a letter from the consular representative. He had discovered which cargo ship—the MV Rong Chen, he said—had sailed from Tiajin the morning she was sent away. The Captain, however, denied Nööne was aboard. *Sometimes we take passengers, that's true enough,* the Captain told the representative. *But I've never taken them against their will. I don't tempt fate. Ships get lost as easily as people do.* (I could imagine his shrug.) *Even a ship as big as the Chen.*

The Captain seemed sincere, the consular representative added. *There's little else I can do.*

He signed off with his good wishes.

There must be a sequel to this story. Because I know I haven't told it right. Because, now, there is only a stone and a street.

Because Nööne is always right.

Today, a car exploded. Near a church. Outside a market. Three men inside. There was a reporter nearby, a tourist caught her on camera as she ran—a basket of fruit in one hand, a satchel of papers loosely held in the other— toward a limp man splayed on the sidewalk. I could not see the reporter's face, but I could tell by her long unbound hair, the curve of her hips, that she was American, that she was on business by the way she held her bag as she stooped to help the injured. The video was shaky because the tourist's hands were shaky, because the tourist was running as he taped the reporter moving from body to body, over torn concrete, a girder, around the hood of a car standing upright in the ground. The tourist swiveled and the lens took in collapsed stalls, the pitted sidewalk. Water erupting from a severed line gushing around his feet.

He did not focus on the woman's face. Only her hands. Hands like Nööne's hands—long, but not tapered or delicate. The fingertips were stained with ink.

I waited. But the camera lens did not rise.

The Religious

Outside the Restaurant Suisse I lay in the ivy. I was flat on my back, the ivy curled around my arms and legs, bucking my chin (tickling me really). A soft vegetal bed. I smelled of shade because it smelled of shade. Of earth, of cool life among leaves, of small stones and the snails beneath them. In the ivy, it is dark and peaceful while I wait for my guests who are touring the city. They have a map (I sold it to them). My maps always lead to the Suisse.

I met Alice and John out on the green where most tourists begin their morning walk above the Old Town in Quèbec City. The city itself is built into a bluff. At the top, the green is well-tended and groomed. From there, the views are exquisite: it's easy to roam down to the walls of the Old Town, it makes perfect sense. Even I begin my day on the green.

At first I didn't see Alice and John, at first I ignored them while they strolled, taking photographs of monuments as most tourists do. John's camera was slung around his neck, his visor tilted up toward the sky searching for signs of bad weather. There were none: the clouds were full, the breeze mild. But he continued to look, continued to pull Alice behind him as though he were hoping the sky would grow smug so they would be forced to abandon their journey. John was sullen—there's no other word for it. Soon enough there were words, a hushed exchange full of spit and nerve that rocked the quiet air with its tension. That's why I turned (I like to watch couples quarrel), that's when I saw Alice's knees the first time. They were perfect and white: astonishing, round. I picked up my maps. I ran to Alice (her knees were that nice). I ran with my arms in the air, the maps aloft, hurrying because, unless I was mistaken, Alice's knees were pointing toward me.

"Hello!" I called waving my hat. "Hello!" until they stopped arguing, were forced to wave back—hesitantly—as if I were an acquaintance whose name they'd forgotten. Then John saw the map in my hand.

"No thank you." He was abrupt, firm, he was turning away. I am used to rudeness (all mapmen must be). It's frequently the first step toward a sale.

"Sir," I chided. "Don't miss out on my offer. Look here," I said unfolding my map. "I have the best map of the city. I've listed the monuments of common interest—the Plains of Abraham, the Citadelle—as well as attractions of a more unique nature: for instance, the abandoned lot on the edge of the Old Town where they feed the carriage horses at dusk. I'm sure the lady would like to see that."

Alice leaned toward John. Her voice was a whisper but I still could hear it. "John, it could be fun." Already, she was on my side. But John hushed her (he was still angry). Then, sighing, he took the map from my hand.

"This map," I went on, "is comprehensive." I smiled. "Better yet, I'll sell it to you for half price." I winked at Alice (I think she blushed). "I give more for less."

"How nice." John studied the map while Alice looked over his shoulder. I waited. I watched them both closely, studying Alice's knees at leisure. I was right: even now as she leaned on her husband's shoulder, her head pressed to his side, her knees were angled toward me.

John remained silent, but after a time, he gave Alice a nod and she pulled cash from her purse.

"You won't regret it," I said as we made the exchange. They didn't answer, they were already gone. Perhaps they didn't hear me.

That sale (the lone sale of my day) had taken place after breakfast. Now the night had pulled a wool blanket over the Old Town, the lamps had flickered to life. Shortly, Alice and John would arrive, I had no doubt. I have lived in Quèbec City for fifteen years, my guests rarely fail me. Tourists follow maps— that is their job. They will follow a map into the sewers.

As if my thinking of them induced their arrival, Alice and John turned up as guests often do—suddenly—even when they're expected. Their arms latched but not locked, they walked up to the Suisse, peered through its windows at the tables within, at the biergarten where I myself dine each evening, and where that glorious bounty of woman—my Rosalie—works each night until ten. In Alice's left hand was the map I sold John. Her right hand held her belly. Alice was pregnant. Why hadn't I noticed before?

Rising, I brushed myself off as they entered the Suisse. I walked in behind them, followed them among long tables shared by groups of strangers. As Alice went for a chair, I stepped on John's heel. He stopped—what choice did he have?—and passing him, I took his seat. I sat next to Alice at the head of the table. What a simple feat to sit between them.

Above the biergarten, the moon glowed red and as one star fell, full of haste, from the sky, I touched Alice's arm. I pointed up through the arbor above us—through lilac and vine to the stars.

When John at last sat down across from his wife, Alice was smiling with the wonder of it. Flushed with a red August moon.

"I am Arnot de L'Oeufs," I said offering up my hand to him. I wondered if he'd remember that I was the mapman. He didn't. I wasn't surprised as he took my hand: he barely looked at me when we first met.

"I'm Alice," she said and stood up. I tried to take her soft hand in my own, but it was occupied elsewhere—plucking a lilac from an arbor above us, threading its thin stem in her hair.

Soon enough, though, I learned they'd been married eight years, that Alice taught poems and John fixed cracked teeth, that they lived in a coastal town outside of Boston. Alice even told me that she was with child, that in five months (she at last gave a hint of her smile) two would finally be three.

"We could not conceive," she confided, her voice at a whisper. "You see, we had to have *help*."

"Congratulations!" I turned and thumped John on the back, but he shook my hand off. Alice watched—she'd gone quite still in her chair. Across the table, she watched us both.

"How fortunate you are," I told them as I stretched my

legs under the table. I might have even touched Alice's knee with my own, let it nudge the soft white flesh of her thigh, but Rosalie—the full mountain of her—suddenly appeared (as she often does) at my side. For a large woman, she is surprisingly swift—her body hovers and crests as she moves between chairs, as she bends and fills glasses with water. Yet for all her volume, she is less a fish than a wolf. Rosalie can always find me: even in the ivy, she can always smell me out.

It's her size that keeps me coming back. I plumb her trails, her ocean depths. She has continents for me to explore. And I do. It's why she keeps me. Her family doesn't understand.

"Arnot." Rosalie acknowledged my arrival in her careful way. Then, as my guests studied their menus, she deftly pinched my ear.

"I recommend the fondue," I suggested.

Rosalie nodded. "It's the specialty of the Suisse."

For a moment, Alice met her husband's gaze. When, with a sigh, he nodded, her mood suddenly lightened and like a school girl she clapped. "Make it for two," he said. "Three," Alice added with flair. The grim air between them had quickly dispersed. Is that not the way with men and women?

I pounded the table in my excitement.

"It's fondue all around," I told Rosalie.

Their eyes were bright as Rosalie left to place our orders.

Two sat before me.

They were two, and though they shared a similar scent—an odor of sweat and the city, of lilacs, the candle's blue flame—they sat apart, the one across from the other while, at the end of the table, I sat between them cut off from the rest of the guests. They were quiet among all the talk at the table, a dam that absorbed the chatter around us about castles and rooms, small overpriced objects, about aching backs and indigestion. Two, they sat back, stretched out in their chairs and, together, looked up through the arbor of lilac and vine at the clouds in the dark, at the wings of insomniac birds pulling wind and stars behind them.

I looked from one to the other as they gazed at each other and finally looked back at me. Alice's hand was resting soft on her belly.

I smiled. I can be quite friendly.

"Yes?" John asked.

"I myself am a parent," I lied. "May I offer you some advice?"

John's reply was smooth but curt. "That's not really necessary."

Alice clearly disapproved of his tone. Without a word, she admonished him with her eyes and, gracefully, cut in.

"Please Arnot," she prodded. "I'm sure we can use all the advice we can get."

Her hand was stretched toward me and, without thinking, I picked it up, took it as an offering. John coughed, but I'm sure it was not a mistake. After all, Alice did not pull away.

"Three years ago," I began, "I moved here from my hometown across the Atlantic, from a region of France off the Bay of Biscay in the southwestern province of Dordogne. Though to your ears I perhaps sound as if I belong to this city, I assure you: I am not Quèbecois."

John shrugged but I held him fast with my eyes.

"There is," I insisted, "a difference.

"I was born in Montignac," I went on, "a small town, not even a town but a village built into the slopes of the Northern Pyrenees. My home is east of Bordeaux and west of Lyon. North of Lourdes and south of Paris. It is small, but we have history—a history preserved in burnt ochre and manganese crayon—a history lost and recovered by children. A history later stolen by men with small tools and large reputations.

"We have the first paintings you see—the great hall of the bulls, the horses, the rhino. It's all there etched in umber and red, traced in earthtones—scarred black—above my childhood home. The hunt remains; it goes on there in the caves in the dark."

"Lascaux?" said Alice. She looked thoughtful. "We intend to go there one day."

I was pleased. "Do you know how Lascaux was discovered? Have you heard the story?" Two shook their heads. I clapped my hands in my excitement. "I was there," I explained, "when it was found."

"Tell us!" Alice laughed. Her enthusiasm was half pleasure, half demand. I could imagine her hanging laundered sheets on a line with the same important energy.

"Of course," I said and, leaning over, straightened the napkin which had rumpled up on her lap.

John laid a hand on my arm and I turned to him.

"Tell us," he suggested softly.

So I cleared my throat: I did as he bade me.

The scent of lilac was flush in the air.

"The night before we found the caverns—Marcel, Jacques, Georges, Simon, and I—there was a storm, the kind of buck green storm that only exists in the mountains after the summer has gone, after the damp days full of flies and sweat have dried up, and the warm waters steeped in the lakes run cold. I always knew that the storms would soon come when, in the late summer evenings, I burned a candle, read by its light (at the time it was Livingston's letters to Stanley), and found myself undisturbed by the flutter of moths, the roll and tumble of their thick wings in the flame. Only then was I sure that summer was leaving, that—already—it was time to tug the hatches down, the knickers up. That, soon enough, my mother would pull out the blankets, leave them at the foot of my bed because the chill when it came would arrive as sudden and fierce as a dog in the night that hasn't eaten for days. And as a child I was prone to sickness.

"A forest summer is like no other, it always protests leaving. Septembers in Montignac are filled with its tantrums. And that summer—it was 1940—we had already had more than our share. I can still remember being caught out in the trees when a bright sky full of cotton and blue went black. Yet the day that Lascaux emerged from the dark (it was the 12th, my mother's birthday) we thought we were prepared. The sky, after all, was gray from the outset. But then at noon, it went green, as thick as crushed velvet. The trees bent, gave in without fighting to the hail and the wind; even the stones rattled. And as my mother rushed me out of the house, I was thankful for the first time that we were poor, that there was empty space in the fruit cellar's shallow recesses where the two of us could hide. I was already ten, but I buried my face in her lap as the wind gathered, the walls trembled. Clutching her musty skirts in my fists, it's likely I cried when the sky broke in half. As if a mountain toppled into the valley.

"I do remember my mother shouting, cursing the wind, the water, the deep shaking earth. Her anger coursed through me like her homemade wine. It was a perilous comfort that—oddly enough—put me right to sleep."

John sighed and looked intensely at Alice. She deliberately ignored him.

"I awoke when she pulled my hair," I went on. "The wind had died down, and we pushed the cellar doors open. Outside, our neighbors' children—Georges and Marcel—were waiting in the yard with their infested old dog. They helped my mother brush the dirt and leaves from her skirt. Then they turned to me.

"'Did you hear it?' Georges asked.

"'You must have,' Simon said as he arrived with Jacques on his heels.

"'Come on!' And then they were running and I was running or, rather, I was trying to run, but my mother had me by the ear.

"'Ten minutes.' Her breath was sour. Then she let me go.

"I ran off through the trees, snapping and leaping over thick fallen branches. I called out to the boys, but they were gone. They were fourteen (I was just ten). Already they ran much faster. Already, they'd disappeared.

"'Arnot!' I heard Marcel suddenly shout. I ran toward his voice though I still couldn't see him. Before me was an enormous pine, its thick shag pointing down the slope I just climbed. It had been toppled by the storm, and the hoary trunk jutted out of the earth above a deep hole—a bunker—that was large enough for all four boys to stand in. Inside, they were waiting for me beneath its fat dangling roots—its brazen moss—from which I had the urge to avert my eyes. I was, as you might guess, a very impressionable child.

"'Jump Arnot!' Marcel shouted and, when I did not, he climbed out of the crater and, much as my mother had done, grabbed me by the ear. With a flip of his wrist, he tossed me, and I landed in the soft earth at Georges' feet. He stood me up, wiped the dirt from my eyes.

"'Can you see?' he asked (sympathetically I thought). But when I nodded, he picked me up, bent me like a broken compass—face down, my small boots pointing sole-first to the sky. He stuck my head, my shoulders, through a dank hole in the dirt. By my legs, he held me upside down in the dark, in an opening at the base of the crater. For a moment, I thought the boys had simply played a trick until I realized that the hole was large and dry, that, inside, I could feel the absence of earth, a fierce plenty of air, stale and abiding around me."

"How cruel," Alice said, shaking her head.

"I was young," I explained, stroking her fingers (I still had her hand). "I never knew my father, only an uncle from Dijon who, like all Dijonais, worked in the mustard factory there and always smelled like sulfur." I coughed. "He rarely came to visit. So you'll understand when I say that I had no precedent for tight-lipped manhood, that I was quite simply scared out of my wits."

"I bet you screamed like a girl," John said.

"I was just a boy," I sighed. "No doubt my voice shook the walls."

Alice squeezed my hand. "Go on," she said, ignoring her husband. I of course obliged.

"'What do you see?' Georges shook me. His grip was tight—alarming—on my thighs.

"'It's too dark,' I pleaded.

"From above, I heard Marcel curse, and then he pressed a lighter into my palm.

"'If you drop it,' he said grimly, 'I will make Georges drop you.'

"Georges shook me again. 'Well?'

"I sparked the lighter, and the flame lit up. A small bit of light, a wink in the dark. But I saw the cave, it was all there beneath me not twenty feet down. I saw the paintings, I saw them all. But I spied the drop too and as my fear once again overcame me, my organs revolted, they loosened—you might say south became north—and, cursing, Georges pulled me up. He dumped me in the dirt at his side."

"For god's sake," John muttered.

I sighed. "It's true. I was weak, and I ran home to my mother. I spent the day cleaning gutters while the boys dug in the woods. Opened the mouth of the crevasse under the pine and explored the cavern below.

"I saw them first, you understand. I saw the bulls and their cows painted on the cave walls. They were nothing more than stick figures—just childish drawings—drawn in red and brown. I saw their horns, the spears and the blood. I saw the horses, I saw it all. I was the one who saw it first."

I gripped Alice's hand.

"Yet on the front page of the paper the very next day, their picture appeared and I wasn't in it. There they were—the four of them—arms crossed and proud, their brown dog at their feet. I scanned for my name, I read the article thoroughly. But did they mention my contribution?" I shook my head. "Later, I tried to clear up their story. That's when I learned at all too young of an age that truth and perception are much different matters. There was my truth, here as I've told it. But the truth couldn't compare with a photograph of four young boys— shirts wrung with dirt—their bodies smudged by the very same earth that once covered our ancestors' drawings. That was what lasted, that's all people now know. Their story became history. It is history now.

"*Now*," I told them, "there's no difference."

There was a long pause and Alice filled it with a frown. "That just doesn't seem right." She was shaking her head. I don't think it's too much to say that she felt sad for me.

John's eyes were bright, however, perhaps even cruel. "At last the moral." He smiled: "Every boy needs his father."

I shook my head.

"If you'll bear with me," I sighed, "there's more."

Did I imagine Alice's look? Was she relieved? At any rate, hands fluttering, she waved me on. Once again, her knees were aimed toward me. An invitation: I had to look away.

"Years passed," I continued, "years without acknowledgment. But I didn't let my young struggles shape me. No: I went on to excel while Jacques, the buffoon, became a mechanic and Simon took a job tending bar outside town; while Georges and Marcel went into business and opened a hotel together. From what I understand, they were successful. At least their guests, and many locals, praised them. Yet, by a stroke of ill fortune, the hotel became infested with fleas (to this day, no one knows how). It wouldn't have been so bad of course had they not catered to certain public officials who made a habit of using the rooms to meet their posies on the side."

I shook my head sadly. "How do you explain to your wife how you've become a nest for vermin?"

"My, my," John said softly. It was almost a whisper.

"You can imagine the scenes," I told him. "Georges and Marcel had to shut down the hotel. They had to leave town shortly thereafter."

"Well done." John raised his glass to me.

I ignored him of course.

"Meanwhile, I went on to Bordeaux, to the University. There I tried one thing and another. First, mathematics, finance, then administration. Nothing, however, seemed to take. Until one day soon after I turned twenty-five, I returned home to visit my mother (she was by then ailing with a disease of the lungs) and I learned that the archaeologists were limiting tours of the caves, that the paintings were in peril.

"That was 1955. By 1963, the caves were closed altogether. Now you can't see the bulls anymore."

Surprised, Alice sat up in her chair, but Rosalie's arrival from the kitchen—not unlike a wave mounting the shoreline—distracted Alice from the past to the present. I lost her to hot porcelain bowls steaming with pastures and maids. I lost her to diced bread and an empty plate that she quickly filled. For a student of poetry, Alice was all prose as she wielded her skewer like a harpoon—dunking her bread in the fondue, then raising it (dripping and hot) like a large and hard won trout. Puckering her bright round lips, she blew, then sucked the bread off the pike.

I whistled in gentle approval, let my knee touch her thigh. I couldn't help myself.

At my side, Rosalie waited; she was waiting, she would wait (I knew her too well). I dropped my napkin, and we went down for it at the same time.

"My place," she said. "Eleven o'clock?"

I slipped my hand inside her blouse. She was soft and I lost my fingers in the warm well of her breasts. Behind her, I could see Alice's knees under the table. She was relaxed, her knees slumped apart. Her napkin was sliding again to the floor.

Rosalie turned and followed my eyes. "Be good."

It was a warning and, leaning on the side of my chair to pull herself up, she stunned me with a blow to the head. It was accidental of course, and not the first time she'd hit me. Her large limbs (she once explained) responded less to her will than to gravitational pull and inertia, the positive and negative charge of apparent ions, all the laws, in short, of physics. They tugged her limbs this way and that (she had little control). No doubt at the moment she stood, the earth suddenly wobbled off orbit, and her elbow responded (as it often did) in a parallel flux.

Fortunately, neither Alice nor John noticed the slip. Alice was eating at an impossible pace while John watched with concern (I gathered the site was not unfamiliar), begging now and again a soft *take it easy* which she studiously ignored.

"Shall I go on?"

Alice didn't waste her breath. There was a nod for me. And before John could protest, I began.

"In 1955, my life changed. The caves—my discovery— were in danger, and so I offered my help to the local diggers. But what did I have to offer when *employees with training*, they said, *were essential?* By then, at the end of my studies, I had no wish to renew my coursework. So, one evening, while I was bathing my ailing mother, I considered my situation, the situation, that is, of Lascaux: how the past, having become suddenly present, was again shut away from the future.

"My mother was asleep, so I left for the tavern. As I walked, the sun joining the pines on the steep green slopes, I saw a young boy sitting out on the curb. He was crying, and I sat down (not too close) by him. He was not the first to be disappointed: the caves had been closed all day.

"Thinking suddenly of Georges and Marcel, of Simon and Jacques, I leaned over, picked up a bit of red stone in the street. I used it like chalk and drew on the sidewalk. Right there on the pavement where the rain later washed it away, I drew my first picture of a Lascaux horse that I'd seen, its four bent legs and red flaring mane, the hooves tucked under its belly in flight like no horse would ever gallop. I am no artist—believe me—but as though my eyes were a pattern through which I could see, I simply traced the horse. I did not, that is to say, *draw* it. Evidently, I've been branded; my memory was stamped the day the cave emerged from the dark, and I—quite alone—saw the first art of our ancestors as I was suspended in the arms of a boy.

"The drawing satisfied the youngster. His tears dried (though his nose still convulsed) and, exchanging my stone for the gift he unwittingly gave me, I watched him draw a bull of his own. It looked a great deal like my horse.

"The next day I withdrew some funds from my mother's account and signed a lease for a shop. That very day, I began to draw pictures of bulls, of horses on stones I found in the woods near my home. It was effortless, can you imagine? The bulls with their oval heads, their bent horns; the cows grazing undisturbed on the plains. I drew them all—even the rhino, the cat. I drew the spears, I drew the hunt. And everything changed. The tourists changed. They came to my shop. They held each rock, each piece of slate in their hands and imagined digging it up from the dirt. They closed their eyes; they breathed in sulfur and soot.

"And they paid me, let's not forget that. They paid me so they could take history home."

John chewed thoughtfully. "You must have cleaned up."

"Within a year," I admitted, "I earned a small fortune, found a wife. I made my reputation."

"You were vindicated," Alice said softly. A pale thread of cool cheese hung from her chin. John bent over and tugged it off.

I nodded. "In 1963, they closed the caves. People were angry. But what could anyone do?"

"I imagine you'll tell us." John sighed and sat back.

"It was not my idea to build a duplicate cave for the tourists to visit—to build the cave they now call Lascaux II. But, between you and me," I leaned in and lowered my voice, "the chief archaeologist came to my shop the week before he announced the project. He looked around at the stones, at the horses and bulls that I'd drawn. He didn't buy anything, but he smiled: there was a great deal in that smile, a great deal of promise. And when the funds were approved to build a cave not two hundred feet below the original site (I helped with a large donation), I was one among several local artists he hired. It was I who repainted one of the bulls for all the public to see."

Alice looked at John. "Imagine that," she said, "an artist at our table."

"I like to think of myself as a historian." I paused. "In fact, with the exception of a few minor changes, my bull is still there."

"Changes?" Alice was absent-mindedly preening.

I laughed. "Aesthetic arguments were predictable I suppose. But between you and me," I poked Alice's side with my skewer, "a fig is a fig no matter how large, or from what beast it hangs."

John pushed the skewer away. His chin had turned pink. The flesh of his cheeks was sucked to the bone.

"I don't know what you mean." He was actually huffy. Had I ever sat so stiffly in a soft-backed chair? It wasn't hard suddenly to imagine John at sixty, his hair gone white, while Alice dawdled, picked up socks, the sports page, around him. Except that I was the old man; John the youth. What had I said to upset him?

Alice watched John as I watched John. She wasn't shocked. Apparently she had seen this transformation before.

"You know," she said softly, too softly, and for the first time I feared her as I fear most women. "You know exactly what Arnot means."

Silently they fought their battle around me. Motionless, I could feel each parry and thrust. They were transparent power: a tree felled in the darkness. The leg thrust up, a hole wrenched clean. A wound made without a weapon.

John's breaths came hard and controlled, but he refused to respond. He just watched her, they watched each other until, without a word, they both retreated—resolute monarchs who haven't yet had to give up terrain.

When John at last spoke, it was to me. In the blue flame between us, his teeth glowed opaquely. Behind them, as though behind a curtain, I thought I could see his tongue ripple and bow like a puppet. I did not trust his grin. "Arnot," he asked. "Where is your wife?"

"Montignac." It was the truth.

"And your business?"

"She runs it with her new partner."

John was quiet for a moment. Then he had to hold back a laugh. "Let me guess," he finally said. "One of your childhood friends?"

"Georges," I admitted, and John leaned back in his chair,

began whistling a melody to himself.

Alice didn't move. She had simply gone still, even her chest was still, as though her breaths—as they emerged from her lungs—had already dispersed within the air they were made of. As though there was no difference inside her and out. John stopped whistling: Alice had his attention. His small victory had passed.

"You can be mean John," Alice said softly, as a matter of fact. Her tone scared him (it scared me). He sat up in his chair, his hand cupped to his ear as though he could not hear her, hadn't understood what she'd said. But Alice refused to elaborate. I watched her napkin slip to the floor. It didn't rustle as it fell, her napkin didn't make a sound.

When Rosalie at last returned, she seemed to be glowing, her flesh full of late evening dinner light, and I imagined—just for an instant—that there was a faint smile about (though not on) her lips. I looked intently but when she caught me staring, I quickly turned (lest an arm fly). Alice too had luminesced, but her heat was all temperature without its expression. Her eyes were on John. As his were on her. As they sat stunned and apart beside me.

"Are you finished?" Rosalie asked. Alice ignored her and our table seemed to be cloaked for a moment in shadow.

No answer from Alice, Rosalie turned to John. He shrugged, and fussed instead with the pots of fondue that, while I told my story, had overcooked on the flame and crusted up with burnt cheese.

"Take them," I said, my hand on her arm. "We've eaten all that we can."

"What of *la religieuse?*" She hesitated as she looked in the pots.

The question distracted my companions from their mutual stupor. They were tourists after all—it's a learned behavior—and they looked to me as if I were their tour guide, as though I could dispense a compact explanation, a bit of Québecois lore they could take back to Boston, tell their friends, their neighbors, even the child they'd soon add to their numbers. Already, they were preparing to reminisce about their adventures. How different the rest of us are.

I remain, however, a generous man. I pointed into their pots.

"The hard cheese there," I explained. "The locals call it *la religieuse.*"

"It's a delicacy," Rosalie added as though in explanation.

"More like a tradition," I said. "You eat it for luck."

Rosalie frowned. "You're a pagan Arnot. It's not superstition." Rosalie took her time. "*La religieuse* is like a prayer of hope."

"It's cheese," John muttered under his breath.

Rosalie stepped close to him and stroked his hair with her enormous hand. "It is cheese," she agreed softly, too softly, and I was reminded (unexpectedly) of Alice a moment before. "But it is also a prayer." She looked both thoughtful and dangerous at the same time. "A prayer one makes of the past."

He was angry, though he tried to conceal it.

"What Rosalie means," I suggested, trying to calm him in my good-natured fashion, "is that even pagans like you and I must sometimes take part in these rituals—rituals that men invented and women sustain—though we no longer believe."

I must have made an impression, because he turned with a sigh and looked at his wife.

Alice was quiet, however, as she picked up her bowl, ran a delicate finger inside its lip. When she spoke her voice was not soft.

"This cheese," she told John, "it's not just the remains." She stared at her husband. "It's a relic. Don't you see, John?" She paused. "It's what *was* and something *new*."

In Alice's eyes there was no pity. She simply watched him take in her words. Her patience was old, it was no longer patience. It had grown, was still growing, like the child inside her. Perhaps they would be born together.

"Look," I said, then took my skewer and used it to poke the dark crust of cheese that had burned on the base of Alice's pot. The skewer punctured it, and fractured a layer. With my fingers, I picked up a thin brown flake.

John studied the burnt remainder as though it were parchment and a lexicon had been inscribed on its surface. He didn't move. He strained in his chair. Finally, shoulders sagging, he bent his head and looked at his hands.

I waited while Alice watched John, studied a place on his skull which still looked lush with dark hair, but which perhaps was no longer as full as the rest. She had frozen, yet the muscles under her face were in motion and, when I looked closely, I had the curious feeling there was a riot going on there under her skin, that her flesh—soft and white, only a little blue—was filled with veins, filled with traffic. That, suddenly, she had felt her own industry of internal commerce and disposal, all the diners and universities, the gas stations and mini-marts going about their business inside her.

Pursing her lips, Alice reached out and took the cinder of cheese. Snapping it in two pieces, she held half to John's lips. For a long moment, they stared at each other. And, then, John at last opened his mouth, revealed his tongue. He had no other choice, of that I'm quite certain. Delicately, Alice placed half of her token in his mouth, half in her own. They had struck a bargain.

"Bravo." Rosalie rubbed Alice's back fondly as she began to clear our plates from the table. She was smiling the way only Rosalie smiles. As if it were a jinx, as if a smile was asking for trouble.

Alice reached for my hand. "Thank you Arnot."

I was confused, but I took her hand anyway as she stood up.

"You should visit Lascaux," I advised her. "Take John to the bulls. At least the bulls you can see. They are not the same, but good enough."

"Yes." Alice was nodding. "But we'll wait to take the child too. Our family should see Lascaux together."

I watched her walk out the door, knees straight ahead. John followed closely behind.

From my seat, I winked at my girl (she loomed not far off in the corner). John had paid my bill while Alice watched. Americans always seem to pay for my meals: that's why I like to have them around.

When I rose, it was ten o'clock. So I went for a nap in the ivy.

On the ground, cool life at my ankles, I waited for Rosalie.

Parcel Post

For days now, they had left yellow stickup notes for each other, the first of which read: *will try delivery again tomorrow a.m.* She found the note when she returned home from work, a bright sticker framed against the deep oak wood of her front door. A package? From whom? she thought. Daughter or ex-husband? A secret admirer? Certainly not a daughter who forgot even her own birthday, phoning home surprised when she received the silk bathrobe and twenty dollars her mother fedexed to her dorm. Not Jack whose thoughtfulness arrived in looseleaf notes penned in his new wife's hand long after the holidays, signing off: *tell Kate I thought of her last week. Regards to you as well.* But a secret admirer? That pushed speculation into fantasy, she thought. Secret admirers send flowers, not packages delivered by rusty men in jumpsuits.

Perhaps this parcel was missent? she thought. *Perhaps it wasn't meant for me?*

Tomorrow, the small mystery would solve itself. Tomorrow, the delivery man would leave the package on her doorstep—as delivery people always did when residents were not at home. It would be best, she considered, if the package wasn't left on the porch where children might see it, might grab it as they stirred the street playing an afternoon round of kick-the-can when they returned from school. And so, pulling a pen from her purse, she added in black ink beneath the delivery person's script: *please leave package at side door, not front entrance if not home*. At the side door, the parcel would be screened from neighborhood children. She'd be sure to find it there tomorrow when she returned from work.

> Mist and rain. Gas lamps light the sidewalk. From beneath their iron hoods, the light shines forth colic, transforming to a sickly yellow the hands holding a parcel wrapped in sackcloth and bound in twine. Turning the sackcloth to bruised flesh already dead or dying. "Baker Street," reads a sign as she walks on hastily in the rain, skipping quickly as though trailed by a lightfooted malcontent. Marble steps rise to a freshly painted door on which a resident's name is printed and preserved beneath a frame. She cannot read the name; humidity fogs the glass. Still, she leaves the package against the door. As she jogs away, the clouds burst and release a torrent. Rain soaks the package.

The following afternoon, she found another stickup note attached to her side door. *Cannot leave package,* the note said, *without signature. Please sign name on back*. She didn't swear. She didn't curse the inefficient personnel whom delivery companies hired. Instead, she pulled the same pen from her purse and, signing the backside of the note, readhered it to the door. I can wait another day, she thought. I became a disciple of patience long ago, gathering its threads in the late night aisles of Stop 'n' Shops, the lobbies of principals and lawyers. With the threads I've knit a cloak—a black cape lined with sackcloth, a hood made from spun wool. She would drape that cloak around herself before she went to sleep.

> She has lost weight accumulated over twenty years. She is sitting up in bed, dressed only in a blue camisole, the lace rides high above her hips. One leg is bent at the knee. The other stretches out before her so that her hips twist and one haunch, barely covered, angles toward an open door. A young boy walks in and sits by her bed. He leans over her, touches her left breast. He must be twelve, she thinks. Don't be afraid, she says when he removes his hand. He nods, touches her with both hands now. She helps him with his shirt.

The next afternoon she found the note still tacked to the side door. The delivery man left it, or never came at all. Still, no package. She looked behind the potted plants adjacent to the doorway. She pulled up the mat; there was no parcel hidden from the neighbors' prying eyes. No package, not even a note with new instructions. Perhaps delivery men were off on Wednesdays, she considered. But the next day, when she returned in the evening, the note was still adhered to the same pane of glass. Disheartened, she checked the oak front door. There, attached to the wood, were two new notes. *Will try delivery again tomorrow a.m.,* the first sticker read. The other: *Delivery a.m, second attempt. Cannot leave package without signature. Please sign back or parcel will be returned to sender.* Apparently, a new delivery man had been assigned to her package, a new man unaware of her correspondence with his predecessor. An honest mistake, she thought, understandable. How could he have known about her request to make the delivery to the side door entrance? Tomorrow, she thought, is my last chance. Tomorrow, the parcel would be returned to sender. How rude that would be, how ungracious and unkind.

She thought for a moment. Then, retrieving a pad of yellow stickup notes from a drawer in her kitchen, she wrote: *please leave package at side door, not front entrance if not home.* She wrote the message several times, then tacked a note to the front door and the side entrance, even the back door and the garage. This time, she thought, the delivery man would see the notes. This time, he couldn't fail to leave the parcel. Tomorrow, she would at last unwrap the package slowly. Tomorrow, she would finally know who had sent her a gift.

> Dusk. In the distilled evening light, she is watching a fence blur outside a train compartment's window, the ribbon of wood posts broken only by the occasional interruption of a farmer or a cyclist resting by the tracks. Next to her sits a man, his face

turned from her as he presses his forehead against the glass. He has brown hair, a sharp nose. His lips are thick, but not full. She calls his name—Jack—and when she touches his arm, she realizes his clothes are made of canvas. That his clothes are blue and that he's wearing a jumpsuit. *What do you see?* she asks. *You,* he says, *in the mirror of this window.* When he speaks, his voice is strange. Its timbre is high, like a woman's.

The next evening, the notes were gone. The delivery man had tidied up for her while she was at work—peeled away the notes tacked to the side door and the front entrance, even the sticker she flattened carefully to the mesh screen on her back door. Even so, there was no package. Instead, a new note was posted for her on the glass at the side door: *The parcel is delayed,* it read. *Perhaps I will leave it tomorrow p.m.* Satisfactory, she thought. This delivery man, he's a pro. He knows what he's doing.

The following morning, before she went to work, she left a thermos full of coffee at the side door behind the potted plants. She also left a note: *Help yourself. Enjoy the coffee and your day.* When she returned from work, the thermos was neatly tucked against the plants and, she noted with satisfaction, a light ring stained its plastic cup. Still there was no package. Just a message scrawled beneath her script on the note she'd left herself: *Thanks for the coffee,* it said simply. *You're very kind. Perhaps your package soon?* The following morning, she left another thermos. This time when she returned, she found a tiny bunch of posies plucked from her neighbor's garden. The flowers were bound with shoestring and, beside them on the thermos, the delivery man left a new note: *Flowers for the woman who cheers up my a.m. route.* Delighted, she chuckled. Then, filling a tiny vase with water, she set the posies on her kitchen table so she could admire them while she ate.

> Below her window, a fierce arbor of grape vines has grown in the middle of the night. She did not plant them: the vines are only visible at dawn as the light moves discretely over their broad leaves. Climbing out her window, she perches on one gnarled branch. Against her body, the vine is warm, as if beneath bark there's vein and sinew, the novelty of bone. She leans into the arbor: around her, the grapes are sweating; the air is thick with their humidity. She reaches for one dense cluster. But as she stretches, the light shifts. The vine disappears. Her yard is green and neatly mown.

After several days, she had collected an impressive correspondence of stickup notes and, adhering each yellow square to the kitchen wall, she arranged them according to date and day as though they formed a calendar. After one month, the stickup notes formed a yellow window in her kitchen. In three, the window had become a paper door. By the end of the year, there were several such doors throughout her house and, through them, she would often come and go.

The Search for
Anna Boubouli

Anna B.

Who is she, this Anna Boubouli, bouzouki player extraordinaire, street musician and lover of birds, all creatures which sing, especially those which sing out of tune? From Elim, I had heard of her. Sitting beside him at the fountain where we often meet, where we play tunes for coins, for our suppers, he had said without greeting: I have heard a bouzouki mistress. A bouzouki mistress, you understand, because she plays masterfully and without mastery. She plays too many notes, she plays all of them, without a care for the single sheared note that hums an infinite hum.

He stopped then, and the fountain spray misted our necks, wet the flute case by his side. He had not yet played, I could tell, he had been sitting—just sitting—with a wet neck, a wet flute case in the heat. And so, when he added—Perhaps I will play tomorrow, perhaps tomorrow I will play—I knew I had to find her, the Anna Boubouli he described. For no reason, then, for every reason, I picked up my instrument and left him there, and was shortly on my way by bus to the corner where he told me she gathered an improvised band of kettle drums, gravel and tin can tambourines, even a flutist or trumpeter. Each day the music was different, because the band was different. Only the bouzouki remained the same and Elim could not forget its sound, how Anna Boubouli had played.

She is archetypal, he told me. Not the stuff of legend or myth, but a consolidation of her own presence, the presence of music, the absence of music among the everyday. To hear her play was a listening, they were the same. It had made him long to hear her again; it made him avoid her. (It made him try to prevent me from going.)

She is just too much, he tried to explain, she won't reach out and play for her listeners. She is all of her self, her music is selfish, it is too much Anna Boubouli. And why would anyone want to hear that?

Then he paused and, somewhat strangled, said: To hear her makes you realize you ought to be listening more, not just hearing as you've always heard, but listening for something lost or slowly fading out; desire, the lust for listening. Perhaps for sitting still.

Here he stopped, at a loss, he simply couldn't go on: Elim didn't know what it was he was missing. Instead he laughed uncomfortably and picked up a thick book at his side, a bright book filled with words which looked awfully squat, awfully stunted.

There's been a swindle, he said, tapping the cover.

And so, with his nose in the binding I left him there, flute by his side. I went off to find Anna Boubouli.

As yet, I hadn't found her. It was as if, here, where it was known that she played, no one had heard her name or her music. The shopkeeps I asked, the men selling gyros, cucumber seeds stuck to the backs of their hands, not one of them claimed to know her. Anna Boubouli? they said, as though the name were foreign to them, as though they never heard her music, when I knew for a fact that she played nearby. Perhaps just around the corner.

Yet no one could help. I was helpless and where was Anna Boubouli?

By Elim's account, she should have been playing right where I was leaning against the backside of an old and gutted building. I thought the search would be easy. That I would step off the bus and hear the rattle and flock of her strumming, the clatter of people as they threw their change, of children singing. I thought at least her neighbors would know her, know Elim's bouzouki mistress, a woman he described as a most inimical stringer. Yet, it wasn't her music which drew him at first. But her hands, he told me, the way she gripped the bouzouki's thin neck, plucking and strumming indivisible chords up and down the scales. Anna Boubouli was one with her instrument. He could see she played it well, he could tell that from a distance. But the passing buses, the general static that is city noise, had prevented him from hearing a note until he stood up close. And so he had come, and so he had sat, and then he had heard. Then, in much the same way, he left. He put behind him the sight and sound of her rock and sway, and he hadn't been back since.

Of her music itself, Elim said little, other than that Anna B.'s notes were not notes at all, but something like songs in themselves. Each note was a music, not about song, not about what he called the "larger scheme": how a music should make one *feel*. All in all, he said, as though summing her up: Anna

Boubouli remains a plastic animal. But when I pursued this, he had backed off, grabbing his bright book in defense, turning his eyes away.

What I mean, he had said, is that she is difficult. That she is too difficult, not just her music, although her music is difficult. But that she is difficult, that, even worse, she chooses to be so, and her difficulty remains the chagrin of her family and friends.

And why would she want that? he said, and looked at me and was wet.

Her family had passed by her in the street while he was there, Elim went on, an old woman and a young man who he soon realized were the mother, the husband. They stood by her, a little way off, the mother weeping, the husband looking stern at his feet as though he could not look on his wife. But when Anna Boubouli stopped to catch her breath, to rest her fingers for a moment, his voice was soft as he said:

Anna, why not come home? Why play here on the corner where no one will listen? No one at all. We liked your songs, we still dance to them, the songs you danced to when you were a girl. The ones you played when we first got married. Come Anna: you are still a girl, you haven't changed. No one really can change, the girl we know is still in you. Come with us. We love you. (They were persuasive, said Elim.) Come play for us and we will tell you how well you play because we know that you play well.

She wouldn't leave though, Elim told me. Anna Boubouli listened but did not leave, and, quietly at first, the band began to play again, growing louder as the kettle drums rattled and the tin cans shook, until a piper swept the birds up into a bird song, which the piper said later he could not repeat. And no one could tell him how the song had been played because no one had stopped and Anna's family had left. There were no listeners except Elim and the birds pecking his feet, and even Elim couldn't remember because there were too many notes.

And though the birds might have told, they refused.

ELIM

Recently my wife changed her name. Once, we were Elim and Anna Boedeck. Now we are Elim Boedeck and Anna Boubouli.

I still call my wife Anna since I've always called her Anna. She doesn't insist that I call her Anna Boubouli at home, since that would be awkward, it would be inconvenient. Why say: "Anna Boubouli will you please pass the salt?" when "Anna will you pass the salt?" is enough. When a name is short, there are fewer sounds. There is less need for stretching the tongue to get to the rest of the sentence, to get what it is I might need.

My wife has agreed, though she continues to refer to herself as Anna Boubouli. She leaves messages from Anna Boubouli, she signs her documents with her new name—all of it—even letters to friends. She writes it the way she says it, as if it were all one word. In fact, before it became common knowledge that my wife had changed her name, her clients, her friends, began to address letters to her in much the same fashion. So, for a time, my wife's name was Anna Boedeck. Later, it became Annaboubouli Boedeck. Now at last it's Anna

Boubouli as she prefers. We've all grown used to it. You must grow used to things when you don't understand them. Or, as in my case, though I understand why my wife changed her name, I can't conceive why she left—that is, why she continues to leave, swinging back through our home and into our bed, it seems to me, just so she can swing back out again. She's cyclical my Anna. That's all I can say for certain. And I've grown used to that as well.

We met at music school, Anna and I. She was, then, what they call a prodigy. She could play music. Any music—a sonata, a school song, an improvised march, even a twill-hipped swing. She could play them all, with any instrument no less. It was just a matter of one note, then another for her, like walking, but no one could keep up with her pace. Except me of course. I am, after all, what they call a prodigy too. I have, simply, outgrown it.

One can only have so much music, I've told her.

But how much is so much? my Anna would say. More is more. Less is less. That's a fact. But: less is more? That's just cake, Elim, for soft bellied cranks who sit around all day. It's stamina we're really talking about, you can see that, you need to build up some. Just a few sit-ups, perhaps, and, tomorrow, so much becomes so much more.

Anna is like that. She eats sweets the same way, too many of them, pushing on past the twinge in the tooth, in the gut. Always pushing on, whereas I invariably feel sick. Most people feel sick. But not Anna. What is enough? she's been known to ask. She still asks it. In this way, she hasn't changed.

In many ways, she hasn't changed. After all, we still play

together. By the fountain, in our kitchen, it's the playing not the place that's important. We played the same way when we were in school, every day in fact. And perhaps because I was the one who kept up, she married me. We kept playing too, but I played less, I just played with her, for her, not for myself. I loved her, you see, and she loved me. As I told her, my love was my playing, to which she'd say—no, your love is your love—and then kiss me.

Which is to say: we understood each other, we were happy.

But then one day she began leaving. My Anna became Anna Boubouli.

I will try to explain what happened. I will try to explain what happened as one writes a story because if a story has a beginning, it may also have an end.

The Later Strummings of Anna B.
by Elim B.

Anna and I, we have a friend. His name is Dahd Vid and he's a strummer like my wife. He plays the fiddle and guitar, but most of all he's known for the large shoes he wears, always one size too big: for growing into, he says, though he is all grown. He's also known for his love of yams, real yams as he puts it— the fleshy New Guinea tubers that weigh several pounds: those are the yams that he loves. Dahd Vid cooks them, then slices them up as one slices a melon, manhandles a piece from the whole. Then he nibbles, Dahd Vid nibbles yam most of the day.

Except when he's playing. Dahd Vid nibbles and plays and trips over his shoes. It's why Anna and I like him.

At any rate, Dahd Vid woke up bored one morning. It was an uncomfortable feeling; Dahd Vid, after all, is not often bored, he's a man of unusual energy. And so to cure himself, to rid himself of the feeling, he quickly dressed and left his home, deciding, as he locked his front door, that he would take the first bus that came to his stop wherever it was going. And so he waited, and when a bus came he rode it to a corner where he dismounted, ordered a coffee and sat on a bench, and began to wait again, looking around for something to catch his eye, something, as he said, unusual. The corner itself was of little interest. It was a hot day and there were few people out walking. Most of them, in fact, sat slumped on their benches looking down at their feet: it was that hot even in shade. In such heat, flesh turns peculiar, he told me. It becomes luminescent, it glows—so much glowing—that one must squint to see.

Dahd Vid, however, is a patient man, and so he continued to wait, slowly drinking his coffee through a straw, squinting as he stared at his feet; above all, ignoring the statue nearby his bench which had been dedicated to unknown poets.

The fate of all poets really; Dahd Vid was unimpressed.

It was then he decided he'd had enough. He was drained: it takes a great deal, after all, to defeat boredom he said. And so, Dahd Vid, sleepy because of his boredom, because of the sun and all the glowing bodies around him, he took off his shirt and, laying down on the bench, propped it under his head. He closed his eyes. He watched sun spots burst behind his lids like yams exploding in the dark. Dahd Vid didn't sleep; he merely rested. After all, one can't really sleep in the city, especially outside on a corner, on a bench without one's shirt, surrounded by glowing bodies. It was while he was resting, then, that he first began to hear the music, not just any music, as he explained, but a most unusual music coming from a place nearby. The band was around the corner, down the street, behind the thick stone walls of the warehouse behind him. He could tell little from his bench. But it was like nothing he'd ever heard.

He rubbed his chin, then paused, before he told me slowly: Elim, it sounded how music sounds when you remember it later, not while it's playing you understand. My friend, it was music which, once heard, sounded remembered. What do you make of that?

It made him feel dizzy, Dahd Vid went on, even though he'd been flat on his back. It made him feel as if he might fall off his bench, onto the pavement and the pigeons there. And so, he held tight to the slats, he wrapped his hands snugly around them. And when, unexpectedly, he heard a bus pull up by his side where the other had dropped him less than an hour before, he scrambled up its steps and into a seat. For the second time that day, he rode an unknown bus wherever it might take him. Not to escape the music, of course: it was lovely, perhaps too lovely he said. But to get home. To prevent himself from falling onto the pavement, onto bird droppings still wet in the heat. But once the bus pulled away, he could no longer recall how the music had sounded, he couldn't remember its notes, its rhythms, as though a music which sounds imagined can't be remembered; it can't be imagined. As if such a music can only be heard.

It was frustrating, he said.

The next morning, then, he took the same bus back to the corner. There he ordered a coffee and sat on the bench; he hoped to hear the music again. Dahd Vid waited. He waited a long while, he said, though he wasn't wearing a watch. He waited. He waited longer. He waited and watched the bodies that glowed in the heat become solid again, become thick as the sun settled down, as the shade became dusk, and the shadows, night. And still there was only traffic and chatter, the fat sighs of gorged pigeons. At last, then, he asked the vendor who sold him his coffee if she had heard music—a most unusual music—as he had the day before. But the coffee vendor just turned away.

Restless, then, he'd gone searching. He left his bench and the corner. He asked sellers of spice, linoleum salesmen, upholsterers beating fabric out on the sidewalk, if they'd recently heard music they couldn't describe. Some had said yes. Some had said no. Others had said nothing at all.

It was hot, Dahd Vid told me. And who wants to talk in the heat.

In the end, Dahd Vid didn't find the bouzouki band. He did find where they played, however, or, rather, where he thought they played, the spot where they must have played, because there was a large sign taped to a wall and the sign taped to the wall said in large letters: Anna Boubouli! It was the kind of sign, he thought, that a band might put up if they'd played in the street so that passersby would know their name, tell other people about them. Which is to say, Dahd Vid left happy because of the sign. Although he hadn't found the band, he at least knew their name. For the time being, it was enough. He would find them again: Dahd Vid would find Anna Boubouli.

Before he went to find her, however, he came to see me. I should say us, but Anna B. was not at home, she was out by the fountain playing her cello, playing for coins, for our suppers. She was waiting for me. I was late. I was even later after Dahd Vid stopped by.

I have heard a music, he said, that I can't describe. Having heard it once like a memory's heard, I can't remember it now. I can't remember it, you understand, as though I never heard it at all.

I must admit I was intrigued. How could I not be intrigued? So, after he left, after he went home to his supper, I wrote a note to my wife. I left it on the table, and then I too went to find Anna Boubouli.

I took the same bus Dahd Vid took to the corner where there was a statue and pigeons—their blinking eyes, their feathers, their necks swiveling in the late afternoon heat. A late afternoon which soon became evening as I sat there watching—listening—my hands on my thighs. Listening for a music I would know when I heard it, because a music that Dahd Vid cannot describe is enough of a description for me. Dahd Vid had piqued my interest (there was no other reason for going). I'm often bored, I'll admit it. As my professors used to say: I am not inspired. Yet, suddenly, I felt overcome. It was rare and so off I went.

After a time, I heard it. It was a strumming, all strings, so many strings; a bouzouki, I was sure of it. And then there were drums, and the sound of a pipe and even a rainstick, and I knew at last what Dahd Vid meant, why he said the music seemed imagined, that Anna Boubouli's music was unreal in a very real way, which meant it was both, that these were the same, and I too felt dizzy and had to sit down. You can't hear such music for long.

For the first time, I understood my wife's words: more is simply more. I knew what she meant. Then came the feeling I've had everyday since: I could feel my own stomach, all of its parts. It was that rare feeling you get when you suddenly realize your guts are made up of slippery chromos held together by context alone.

And I knew things would change as, in fact, they have changed. I knew it was the end.

So like Dahd Vid, I packed myself onto the first bus that pulled up to my side. I needed to leave. I could no longer bear Anna Boubouli's strummings.

I came home to a wife who played alone for a supper which, while I was out, had grown cold. It was a supper I ate slowly, then left on the table. Anna B. of course thought I was sick (I was sick in fact). So she nursed me: she bathed my head with a cloth, whispered soft nothings I knew she would no longer whisper if she were to hear of Anna Boubouli. And soon she would. There are some things a husband knows, and I knew this without a doubt: Anna Boubouli would find my wife if my wife didn't find Anna Boubouli. That's why I was sick. Because my wife, Anna Boedeck and I—we—were going to change.

There are some things, after all, a husband can't keep from a wife. Though I tried to keep Anna Boubouli from mine. But the next evening when Anna B. found me by our fountain, the fountain where I had been sitting—just sitting—because I could not play, because I had heard an inimical stringer and, like Dahd Vid, forgot her sound too, my wife saw my trouble. She knew something was up. She's my wife after all and, being a wife, she asked me what was wrong.

Some things a husband can't keep from his wife, and I could no longer keep back this:

I've heard a bouzouki mistress, I told her. She wasn't a master, her playing was lousy; it's stopped me up, I can't play.

But Anna Boedeck, she saw through me. There is little one can hide from a prodigy, especially a prodigy who is also your wife. So, I told her the rest of the story, at least what I knew of it. And then Anna B. packed up her cello as I had foreseen. She left me sitting on the ledge of a fountain with a flute case that was wet. She left me reading a book.

What's it about? she asked before she departed.

There's been a swindle, I told her. Then she left.

What's a husband to make of that?

ANNA BOUBOULI

Who is she, this Anna Boubouli, sidewalk strummer and lover of tunes, of ineffable strings and passersby who ignore her for all her trouble? About her, at least one thing is clear: she demands a matter of seeing, a metre of hearing. In other words, she's much like a prayer—and a girl tends to be attached to her prayer, what might be called her neigh.

One might even say, her name is a story:

A GIRL AND HER TOOL

by

Anna Boubouli

née Annaboubouli Boedeck

née Anna Boedeck

née Anna B.

née née

When Anna B. left Elim at the fountain, she didn't simply go looking for Anna Boubouli. She went to play with her, play the cello, even though she can play any instrument at all. It's just the cello she prefers, it's the instrument she loves, and one must love one's instrument. You see, Anna B. can play the bouzouki; the bouzouki and the cello aren't really that different, though the sounds they make are distinct enough. The bouzouki is anxious—joyous and suicidal in the same note. The cello, on the other hand, is like a thick woman who has lived, who has born many children and watched them leave home. Anna B. has no children. She has a cello. And though they are not the same, for now the one takes the place of the other.

In her time, Anna B. has been called a prodigy. That is, she once was called a prodigy, but she didn't play the songs that she should have. She was difficult. That's what her professors said, what her mother told her too. Why are you difficult? they would ask her. Why not play what we want to hear, what your listeners would like to listen to? Why play at all if no one will hear you? And they were right, no one listened. But she kept on playing anyway, in her basement at night with only silence for company, though silence, as some know, can be a very large companion indeed. It must be fed, it must be filled.

Anna Boubouli would understand, Anna B. thought. It's why she had come to find her. Why she needed to play with her.

And so she had come, and so she had searched, and now she was sad. Because there was no Anna Boubouli. Because Anna Boubouli was difficult and no one had listened. Because no one could tell her where Anna Boubouli might be. Where a cello player might find her. Because Anna Boubouli played too many notes for listeners to bother listening.

And as Elim has been known to say: Why would you want that?

For no reason, then, for every reason, Anna B. unpacked her cello right there on the corner, she found her seat on a stoop, and set herself on it. She arranged her cello between her knees and, slowly at first, began to play. Because, when you get right down to it, one must play, and play for oneself. Because there is nothing else to be done.

No one stopped. The passersby, after all, didn't like her playing. There were too many notes and the notes that they liked weren't built for a melody—for a song like the ones they'd heard before: the ones they let flow through them, over them, as is commonly said. When a song, if it's got any spunk (as Anna B.'s often told Elim) ought to clout you, clock a call to attention. In effect, wake you up. But then, as they say, this is a dream world we live in. And we would all much rather sleep.

Anna Boubouli would know that too.

But Anna Boubouli was probably gone. If she did play, why play in the same place over and over, especially if no one is listening? Why not travel? Why not take one's music around the corner, around the country, for that matter, around the world, so that at the end of each day one might know for a fact—no one has listened—with absolute clarity. Because (sighing now) there is always hope. That someone, sometwo, might sit down and listen if only to catch their breath. Perhaps even smile because Anna Boubouli would smile. As Anna B. would have smiled as well.

After a while Anna B. saw a young man at her side. He sat down, there was a small pipe in his hands. He made it himself, Anna B. thought, carved it from what looked to her like the piping of an undercarriage, the junkyard remnant of a car. He tapped his foot, and when she nodded to him, he began to play along. Later there was a girl with a necklace which she put in a can and began to shake. Then a fellow with glasses who thumped out a rhythm on the bruised belly of an old canvas drum. And still people passed. And they were playing and smiling and Anna B. was sweating and laughing. Then, at last, there was the sound of strings from the top of the stoop on which Anna was sitting—a bouzouki's song, she could tell, without having to turn around. And still she played on and they all played on and no one stopped to listen. Yet not because of this, but in spite of it, they went on playing: after all, one must play when one hears such music, play until one has to stop playing because there is nothing else to be done.

When it was finally over, after the shopkeeps locked up their doors and shackled their windows, after the man with the gyro across the street turned off his spit and wiped his counters clean, then finally they stopped, let the instruments hum till they died. And then the woman with the bouzouki stepped toward Anna B. She kissed her on both cheeks.

What is your name? she asked.

And so Anna B. told her:

My name is Anna Boubouli.

The bouzouki mistress smiled: I've been looking for you for a long time, she said. Tell me, where have you been?

I Cook
Every Chance

That spring, the Kaspars lost their possessions the way
trees lose their leaves in the fall. The house keys were first
to disappear. Then flashlights, receipts. After dinner, Pina's
sharpest knife went missing. Ham lost his driver's license
the following day. Within a week, the boys lost their books.
Their backpacks were sitting beside them as the school bus
bounced. The boys and books went up together. Only the
boys came down.

Each night, Pina lay in bed waiting for her things to disappear.
She didn't question the losses. Instead, she gathered her most
precious belongings—the first lock of hair cut from Milne's
scalp, Bobby's infant toenails. A stone Ham once found in the
surf. His only silk tie, a typewriter key. To these she added a
stack of photos which, behind shadows and thumbprints,
documented her marriage. She hid the collection in a crockpot.
The boys would never find it there.

"I'm making dinner," Ham said when Pina arrived from work
one night. He was using the crockpot, steam rose from its rim.

"The boys?" she asked.

He stirred the pot, wiped his lip with his shirt.

"They were gone when I came home."

He ladled the soup into their bowls.

The broth was clear except for Milne's hair and Bobby's nails. Pina's photographs julienned into slivers. Ham had smashed the type key to bits, stripped his tie down to threads. Pulverized the stone into a fine, edible grain.

They sipped the broth slowly. The sliced photos slipped over Pina's tongue, the type bits chimed against her teeth. By the end of the meal, only the grain was left. Tilting the bowl over her lips, Pina let the gritty powder run down her throat. It collected low in her belly, a heap of wet sand into which her life settled. Newly buried like shells at low tide.

Sweetbreads

August 10, 2003

From the will of Joachim van Hoeckel

I bequeath my estate to that so-called novelist, Oskar Heck, whose accomplishments amount to little else but wasted time with ink and ribbon, pages banged out on a typewriter he salvaged from my attic. As I have no other suitable heir, the lot is his—with one proviso: Mr. Heck may secure my savings if he agrees to serve a three month term as sole manager of Hoeckel's Meats (647 Bevel Street, Hoosick Falls, NY). I am fully aware that Mr. Heck has no interest in the butcher business (see attached letter of 3/12/99)[1]. Yet it seems only fair that he operate the store which, after years of toil, generated what amounts to my life savings, a modest estate. If Mr. Heck completes his managerial term without assistance (without advisors, consultants, counter and office employees) much as I did, and does not run the business into the ground (forecasted margin of error is +/- 6% of 2002 taxable income) he may without penalty inherit my estate. During the three month

---

[1] Father,
    I will not be a butcher.
    You cannot *make* me butcher.
OvH

period, he will be afforded an allowance and enjoy full access to my home. At the conclusion of his term, my lawyers will evaluate his record.

SEPTEMBER 1, 2003

Oskar found the note at dawn. The slip of folded paper had been carefully worked into the door of the shop so it wouldn't flutter away on the breeze. The paper was crisp and white. Slick, he noted. Wax paper. The words were written neatly in pencil, but the lead had only imprinted the wax. He had to tilt the note in the glare of the lightbulb in order to read what it said.

"Oskar," it read, addressing him by name as though the author knew him, "come to the convent at dawn. Drop off the package on the porch, in the bin in the corner (you can't miss it), just like your father always did." There was no salutation. The writer had simply signed the letter "Sr. Joan Mary of the Immaculate Heart."

Oskar had never met a Sister Joan, although he knew the Convent well. When Oskar was ten, he had been enrolled in their school (the only boy among halls of girls). It was a busy, unsettling, year. His family had moved from Austria just a few months after his mother died from cancer. Just one week after the funeral, his father had already sold his shop, their home, and given his mother's cat to a neighbor. With little warning, Joachim moved his son and his business—all that he had— from Vienna to New York.

Now, at the age of thirty-four, Oskar unlocked the door to his father's shop. He was a virtual stranger; he couldn't remember the last time he stood at the counter or rested his hands on the register's keys—nor what he said the last time he spoke to his father in person. Ten years had passed: by now, there were few people in Hoosick Falls who would recall he was his father's son. Oskar had put on weight, he'd moved away. He had even changed his name.

September 2, 2003

Morning

Not long before dawn, Oskar rolled out of bed, tugged his boots on, and made his way to Bevel Street to prepare the Sisters' package much as his father had for twenty years. First, he awaited the delivery of freshly slaughtered stock. Then, as his father once taught him, Oskar began secondary slayings, carving the new carcasses into roasts, ribs, and steaks. He followed his father's methods precisely: purchasing an animal split by the dealer, then slicing up the beast himself. *Bones*, his father often had told him, *they're the key to texture and flavor.* Pre-packaged meats? (He'd scoff, shake his head.) Joachim refused to sell them at the store.

Oskar was ten when his father opened the butcher shop in a neighborhood on the fringe of town where the rents were more affordable. At the time, the shop was small. Joachim specialized in sweetbreads; in livers, tongues, brains, and eyes, gonads and intestines. Organs the town market never had on hand. The first day the shop was opened, their patrons seemed to arrive like hounds. Nose up. Following the scent of fresh blood on the breeze. Taking Joachim aside, they quietly admitted that for years they'd had to quell the urge for the viscera of beast and fowl alike. Abstain from thoughts of satisfaction by reigning in the carnivores inside them.

To all of this, Joachim sighed and nodded; he could be eminently reassuring when a profit was at stake. Even when the Reverend Mother first came calling, he provided her with service unexpected in a man who could parse a steer like grammar—into its proper parts. He didn't tell her that he had no god, that blood had become his bond, almost a religion. "It's in fish and bugs, in beasts and men," he'd say. It was shared, it could be shared: Joachim bent his head at every meal to honor the blood he spilled.

"Mr. van Hoekel?" The Reverend Mother's flat, inquisitive face was pinched as she ignored Oskar at the register and leaned across the counter.

"I have a proposition for you," she went on when Joachim emerged from behind the butcher's block, wearing a dirty apron. Without flinching, she took his hand when he offered it, and they went together back to his office. How tough she was. *Sturdy,* Oskar thought. Built equally from fat and muscle. Knocking cases with her broad, square flanks as she made demands. They spoke for over a half hour. And in the end, they shook hands one more time: Joachim had agreed to donate a weekly ration of meat—as much as the Sisters required—in exchange for prayers for his dead wife and his only son's education.

"It's a bargain," he told Oskar. And then went back to work.

Soon after, young Oskar was admitted to the convent school. He wasn't unwelcome—there were so many things a boy could do while the girls went to study hall. Oskar's lone pair of pants in fact rarely garnered attention among the crowded skirts of his peers: their sights were set outside the gates at the boys who gathered after school, not the queer egg who had hatched among them. Certainly, the girls were kind. But most often Oskar sat alone. He knew there was talk among them about the scent of dried blood that clung to him—a stale perfume, like history—that he simply couldn't shake. He tried soaps and creams. And when those failed, onion skins and garlic. In the end, the girls ignored the smell by ignoring him. But they always blamed him for the heavy vapor of simmered meat that greeted them each morning: it rose from the convent's kitchen as they arrived for class each day, the scent filtering through a maze of vents—into classrooms and confessionals, inside lockers, throughout the gym. By 9am the air was thick with the Sisters' lunch of roasted pork. Sausage stew. Soft, over-boiled potatoes. Twenty years later, Oskar still associates the thought of open schoolbooks with the smell of bloated, bursting meat cooking over a flame.

August 7, 2003

A Eulogy for Himself by Himself

Joachim van Hoeckel ran his butcher shop in Hoosick Falls just like his old store in Vienna. He had rules, maxims, and he kept to them. Then he taught them to his son. 1.) Never let a dealer bone your meat. 2.) Always make your cuts yourself. 3.) Only buy fresh fowl. Stretched side by side, the birds arrived in cardboard boxes naked of their feathers. Rabbits turned up much the same way. Then into the shop's cold case, they went together: prime grade meats of beef, lamb, and goat—pig, from hoof to snout.

Joachim had expectations and he met them. Though occasionally, when no one looked, he used his thumb to tip the shop's scales to his favor—a gentle list and pull was enough to do the trick. Yet Joachim never overcharged his clients more than an eighth. Even in deceit, he was modest. Just as a working man ought to be.

For twenty years, Joachim kept his promise to the Convent, long after Oskar earned his degree, left him, left home, even left the store. Mostly, he sent them pork butt (pig *shoulder* the nuns preferred to call it). Intestine casings. Sweetbreads. Never lipid cuts. In fact, in all that time, only a few deliveries had been second best—tallow or perhaps over-tough—and those he'd ground up for them, spicing the meat heavily with sea salt, basil, and fresh peppers: "a specialty," he said. If the Sisters noticed, they never complained. Not even when Joachim began to charge for intestine casings after Oskar passed his last exam. The gut was expensive, after all. And Joachim worked it by hand himself. Stripping the intestine of its lining, he made sure the cleaned, trimmed casings were bound securely, delivered moist. The casings rarely burst: it was unusual, even, to find lethal pinpricks in them through which their contents could spill out.

SEPTEMBER 2, 2003
STILL MORNING

Oskar walked quickly to the convent, heaved the package against his hip the way he'd hold a child, giving it time to adjust—flesh on flesh—just like a tiny body would. He had forgotten that at dawn even a small town isn't silent: he could hear trucks roaring on Route 7 out from Albany or perhaps back from Vermont, his own soles scuffing pavement; even the dim twitter of birds in nests. Already the town was humming. Yet when Oskar turned up the Convent's drive, the world suddenly went silent. Old enormous evergreens shrouded the building from the street.

The Convent of the Immaculate Heart was a fierce and stately structure. The pendant was supported by four thick columns behind which two massive iron doors (drawn by an old winch and chain) opened up into a foyer with a marble chapel just beyond. The Sisters' rooms were located on the upper floors designed, like a horseshoe, to wrap around the first floor chapel, so that, while the faithfuls' souls were trained inward, their windows faced out on the drive. Oskar was careful to be quiet as he made his way up the front steps to the landing, each breath soft, hushed, though he was winded by his quick pace at dawn. As promised, he found the metal hamper to which Sister Joan referred. The lid squeaked as Oskar pried it up. Protested a second time as he left the pork and sausage casings, a large roast, inside.

Oskar hovered by the bin, wondering, as he hesitated, if he ought to ring the bell; if he ought to wait for Sister Joan.

He paused. He listened for her. He was unable to shake the old schoolboy memory that, just inside, the corridors were filled with habits. That legs in thick stockings were bent in prayer. Or had just then been roused from sleep.

Shrugging, Oskar left, walked back down the steps. He had reached the drive when a small, seamless door cut within the massive entrance soundlessly swung inward, and an abundant woman sidestepped out, squeezing herself with effort through the tiny frame. Though large, she moved swiftly—she reached the bin before Oskar could take one stride toward her—growing smaller with each step, as though the fresh air had made her shrink. She didn't turn, she didn't even trouble to acknowledge him though he knew, without quite knowing how, that she knew he was there. Against her dwindling body, the packages looked enormous, nearly seemed to topple her. But once back inside the Convent, she seemed to grow large again; her body patched the tiny door, blocked the little light that glowed behind her. When she turned, stooping slightly—perhaps to grab the bolt?—Oskar was afforded one glimpse of her pale face, the white lips pursed together, bangs of brown hair straying out beneath her veil. Without haste— all her movements were efficient—she slipped the seamless doors together. Silently, the latch snapped back in place.

MARCH 23, 1984
CHILDHOOD

In Spring, Bevel Street is dry and cool. Guided by the steep facades of the 19th century brick townhouses (mostly converted by then into apartments, eateries, and novelty shops), the breeze that blows up from the dim waters of the Hudson pulses along the entire street. Drinks in hand, seniors sit on stoops all day, dealing cards on plastic tables. Children bat balls with long sticks. And shoppers roam in and out of stores like Hoeckel's Meats as they walk home from work.

That the Hoeckels lived on Bevel Street was both a source of angst and pride for sixteen year old Oskar, an immigrant in a town of old New Yorkers whose roots were so obscured by time they no longer knew who they once were and resented newcomers for their memories. Yet it wasn't because of his accent that Oskar often found himself sport for local bullies. It was his place at the convent school, as though his proximity to a flock of women made him doubly strange, and they could sense a soft German girl hiding inside him just like the spy he knew they imagined him to be. They smelled her blood on him, they said as they closed in. It's what made them kick him. Send him down hard and fast so they could use their fists. He was only spared when Mary Slingers walked with him. She lived down the street, went to his school. And though she must have known she was his only friend, it never appeared to trouble her at all.

There she was each morning, walking by his window, the socks of her school uniform pulled up to meet her skirt. From his basement window, Oskar watched as she arrived, as she stopped outside his father's door. Her knees grew red as she stood in the cold and, tapping her foot impatiently, her rustling skirt revealed her thighs. Above that, Oskar glimpsed only darkness before the bell jingled and his father invited her in, leading Mary to the office above Oskar's bedroom. Below them, late, he'd listen to their muted voices while he packed his bookbag. Then up the stairs, he'd knock once, twice, on the trapdoor to his bedroom before he pushed it open and his father offered down a hand—pulled Oskar through the floor into the office like a hare out of its den. Then he and Mary were off together: the mornings rarely varied. Half way to school, Mary rolled down her socks, pulled up her skirt. At sixteen, she informed him as she aligned her skirt below her flanks, she'd already had enough of school. There was little else to learn.

It was something to stand beside her, something to be seen with her as they walked by the public school, past boys leaning against old brick walls, waiting impatiently from first bell to last for the school day to be over. Mary was crafty—truly artful—as she walked. She never paid much mind to the boys who leered at her, never spoke to anyone but Oskar until they walked through the Convent's gates. Yet he knew she liked to catch their eyes, watch them struggle not to stare at her. When she bent to tie her laces, she'd stretch one leg forward and flex her thigh, then take her time smoothing her pleated skirt against her hips. Oskar always had the impression, though, that it wasn't her power to tease that thrilled her. It was something else—the palpable taste of almost, but not quite, sex, a kind of constant she sensed all around her, like a salmon swimming against an infinite current in the quest for an unreachable mating ground. Already, Mary understood something she could only articulate many years later: that desire had limits, that to kiss a boy, to love him even, would pale by comparison to the simplest passions she'd imagined in her dreams.

Perhaps it was this prescient schoolgirl awareness that kept her from being pestered, because no one dared to approach her as she walked from Bevel Street to the Convent's grounds with Oskar at her side. There were no cat calls, no propositions, never mind feels copped on crowded sidewalks. Oskar knew that as a chaperone, his efforts to protect her would have been futile. It was Mary's presence that guarded them. Her confidence mocked and defied boyhood. Her outrageous girlish sex compelling just as it simultaneously repulsed.

OCTOBER 5, 2003

LETTER RECEIVED AT THE IMMACULATE HEART CONVENT

Dearest Reverend Mother,

I hope this letter finds you healthy. That you remain sturdy, as full of iron, as I remember from my youth. That the ruler still leaps to your palm.

As a former student (Class of '86) and the new, if temporary, owner of Hoeckel's Meats, I ask your help in the following matter.

It has come to my attention that Mary Slingers, another former student and my old childhood friend, may be living at the Convent. As I lost touch with her under peculiar circumstances many years ago, I ask nothing more than verification of her well-being. If in fact she has joined your number and wishes to see me, however, I would be delighted to enjoy her charming conversation once again.

You may be assured of my discretion.

My everlasting gratitude,

Oskar Heck

(formerly Oskar van Hoeckel)

1991-2003

Any Given Day

During her twelve years at the convent, Sister Joan always woke up early in the mornings to complete her daily chores. No longer the bold girl who grew up "on the Bevel" (as her old street was still referred to), Joan not only had lost the sleekness of her youth, but, more importantly, her impatience—the sense that she was missing out, that the world was a more eventful place than Hoosick Falls could ever be. Now the memory of her youth was like a scar she touched infrequently, but which raised just enough above the flesh, could still remind her of its history with an unexpected brushstroke. Most days she ignored it—at last taking pleasure, even pride, in the woman she'd become. After years of wearing her habit, her body mimicked its A-line flair. Her bosom shook, her muscles flounced. A welter had replaced the firm, quick step for which she was once known. Few people recognized her.

Rising at dawn, she dressed and went down to the porch to retrieve the butcher's package. She didn't bathe. All too soon she would be elbow deep in the delivery that it was her job to grind.

In the kitchen, dressed in her habit, a smock and slippers, she enjoyed working with her hands. They were deft, even graceful, as she sliced the pig shoulder into pieces, fed them to the convent's grinder, and cranked the meat at a steady pace through its iron mandibles. She had to concentrate, focus her mind and arms together. If she stopped, the meat would jam the gears, require her full weight as leverage to make it start to chew again. Her powerful body—Joan delighted in its mass, the authority it gave her. When she sat, her backside enveloped her seat. When she walked from stove to sink, she felt each chafe of her thighs. Sister Joan had become aware of space, the space, specifically, her body *took up*. Her girth gave her presence, made her feel alive.

October 11, 2003

"Nobody Beats Hoeckel's Meat"

Oskar had settled into work at the shop, into the blood and the marrow, the oily acrid scent that infused his clothes, his skin, his hair—a scent he was once accustomed to, but with which he no longer was familiar. After tallying up the first several week's receipts, he knew the shop was doing well, that he was in keeping with his father's will. So hardly an hour after he opened his doors, he decided to take the morning off. He locked the cases, put a note on the door: he promised himself that he'd double his deliveries that afternoon.

In the park, a newspaper folded over one knee, Oskar relaxed on a bench. Pleased with himself, he sipped a cola slowly, watched the cars go by. Is the sun the same sun every day? he wondered, stretching out, looking down over the Hudson, at the current cluttered by beer cans, branches, and small dead fish which had never grown to size. He flipped himself belly-up and studied the sky above him. In the glare, flagellae seemed to swim across his eyes. Oskar could see the bacteria inside him, that part of him even his body kept hidden. Or to which he'd grown so familiar he'd come to just ignore. They wagged their tiny bodies through his optic fluid, kept themselves busy until, this one or that, swam off. Then another appeared. No doubt, he was falling asleep and—too soon—he had to return to work. One more month, he thought. One more. A life. In the city. Worth three months of blood and guts. Chatter over sweetbreads.

MAY 5, 1984
SEX

"Oskar." Mary's voice was sharp enough to wake him in the hours before dawn. She was leaning in his open window, forehead pressed against the glass. Her lips, forming words, seemed disembodied from her face. He could see her teeth, her tongue. He saw how she looked inside, the deep curves of her throat.

"Come out. Hurry."

There was no need to persuade him, he did anything she asked.

Crawling up the stairs quietly, he opened the trapdoor to the office, then slipped out into the alley. When he joined her in the street, he found her on her knees looking down into his bedroom, as if she were studying something there that, for the first time, had caught her eye, and met with her approval. When she saw him, she quickly stood and took his hand. Then without explanation they were running.

There were alleys, short picket fences which they jumped together, steps and stones and puddles, before she led them toward the river's pockmarked banks. He looked to Mary, but her gaze was set down stream where the black current fed the tributary that now was their horizon. When she finally turned, Mary almost seemed surprised that he still was at her side.

"Oskar." She said his name as if it were an answer to a question she did not intend to ask.

Taking him by the hand, Mary coaxed him to a small grove, beyond a clearing that overlooked the river as it dipped and gurgled past large round stones protruding from the surface. In the clearing, there was a blanket spread out on the grass, a water bottle propped against a tree. Oskar paused, but Mary gently pulled him on, as if she knew he could not resist her—that a boy won't resist a girl who knocks for him in the night. He was shaking, though, as she led him by the large, round buttons secured by shop twine to his pajamas. At the blanket's center, she pushed him down, let him go. Let him watch her muster up her courage. Mary breathed in deeply—once, twice. Then she began to strip as quickly as she would at home: as though she were getting ready for a bath and had forgotten he was there.

Mary sat beside him, and beckoned him to take off his clothes. When he was ready, she pulled him to her, rocked him slowly against her breasts until he couldn't help but climb awkwardly above her, lay himself unbalanced between her thighs like a stranded fish upon a rock. They lay still like that, his groin against her belly, their foreheads pressed together as the midnight breeze kicked up. The trees shook, Mary's muscles clenched, and, breathing hard—he could not stop—Oskar pushed himself inside her. He was a living thing, he held onto her, and tried to find the way.

Below, Mary watched him. She watched him kiss her, watched his face first grow red, then turn pale, as he forgot her in a conscious lapse that was his body trying to remember what it had never known. How could she explain to him that he made her feel tidy, neat—that the sensation of him was merely pleasant—as though she were putting books back on their bookshelves in their proper slots? She watched him closely. Even watched herself in the dry reflection of his eyes. Then Oskar clenched and the rest of him followed in a gasp. Inside, she felt stung as the salt of him seeped into her. She winced as he stared down at her, uncertain what to do.

Mary pushed him off her and, as Oskar rolled onto his back, she studied him—wrinkled now—damp with sweat and the insides of her that he touched.

He was silent as he looked back at her. Dead leaves scuttled by them like crabs across the grass.

Reaching for her purse, Mary began searching for the tissues she'd brought with her. She let Oskar watch as she squatted, poured the water down her crotch and, cleaning herself quickly, dried the beads of water that welled around her knees. After, Oskar handed her the clothes beside him. Then they dressed together quietly, as if Mary had brought him to the river many times before. Yet when he was ready, she collected all of her belongings—the blanket, the bottle, the tissues too—and threw them off the bank into the Hudson.

Back in bed—perplexed, confused—Oskar could not sleep. He did not sleep for several weeks it seemed as Mary increasingly became strange with him, even stopped making her morning visits to the store. And then one day, she was simply gone. Mary disappeared from both the street and school. Oskar never heard from her again.

At sixteen, Hoosick Falls was too small. Mary must have had enough.

Once a month, Oskar went to see Mary's parents, went to ask if they'd heard from her. Her father always put him off, hesitated, once slammed the door. So Oskar stopped inquiring. Two years later, he went West for college. And when, after graduation, he returned, it wasn't to Hoosick Falls he moved, but to a studio in Brooklyn. In eleven years, he'd written eleven novels there, while working odd jobs to pay the rent. Meanwhile, the Slingers moved to Rochester. A letter Oskar once sent to their new home never garnered a response.

DECEMBER 5, 2003
HEADLINE, HOOSICK HERALD: "HOECKEL'S MEATS, NEW DIVINE OWNER"
BY MICHAEL STERNE

> HOOSICK FALLS—Hoeckel's Meats, a landmark storefront on Bevel Street, has once again changed ownership since the recent

death of long time proprietor, Joachim van Hoeckel. Van Hoeckel, an Austrian by birth, immigrated to the United States in 1984, and quickly became a popular character on Bevel Street, renowned for telling tales of elaborate proportions. Residents were not surprised, therefore, when he designated young novelist, Oskar Heck, as his successor under the auspices of a highly unusual document that required Mr. Heck manage Hoeckel's Meats for a three month term in order to inherit the estate. Since Mr. Heck's tenure began in September, customer complaints have ranged from inconsistent hours, to hygiene issues (there have been no official public health citations). Mr. Heck was also ticketed for public drunkenness and lewd behavior on October 14. Since van Hoeckel's only proviso was an operating margin of +/- 6% of the shop's 2002 taxable income, and Mr. Heck, according to van Hoeckel's lawyers, fulfilled that obligation, the novelist inherited the estate (valued at $240,000) without penalty on December 1. Yesterday, however, Mr. Heck unexpectedly sold Hoeckel's Meats (half of the estate's value) for the sum of $100 to the Convent of the Immaculate Heart to which van Hoeckel donated considerable sums during his lifetime. Sister Joan, the Reverend Mother's representative, refused to comment on the sale, though she suggested the town should pray for Mr. Heck. Mr. Heck himself issued a statement that he has returned to his former home in Brooklyn, N.Y. where he is now at work on his twelfth novel—a *bildungsroman*, he says, a story of love and adolescence, tentatively titled *Hoosick Falls*. He wished to assure local residents that the novel is a fiction. There will be no reference to town events or people living in H.F.

APRIL 14, 1984
OUTING

Once, Mary watched a pig get slaughtered. Mr. van Hoeckel had arranged a drive "out to the country," and she agreed to go with Oskar (she always liked to leave Hoosick Falls). So on a Sunday morning, the butcher warmed up his old Dodge Dart, and they drove south for an hour to a farm in Kingston. It was only after they arrived that she and Oskar learned that Joachim had made the trip as a favor—to give the new owner (an insurance man until he bought the farm) a quick course in vivisection. By the time their Dodge pulled up the drive, a lethargic sow with ruddy spots was tied to a lamp post, the rope slack while she rooted placidly in a yellow patch of grass. When the sow raised her snout, she often sounded a mournful call to a pen of pigs nearby.

After a hushed discussion (the men each smoked a cigarette as they leaned against a wooden fence), the insurance man fetched a tarp and spread it out. Then, as Joachim pulled out his gear—a pair of hip waders and a slicker—the owner turned back to the pig. The sow seemed quiet as he led her by a rope, then tugged her onto the plastic sheet. Though the tarp buckled beneath their weight, the pig stayed calm, she didn't protest. Didn't squeal, even, when Oskar's father swung one leg over her thick haunch and squatted on her back. The sow only started crying out when Joachim pulled his knees together—braced himself—then pulled a shop knife from a deep pocket in his coat.

Oskar turned to warn her. But Mary guessed what was in store. Already, a hand was cupped against her mouth, her jaw beneath it, slack, as she watched the two men, large and incongruous, wrestling with the sow. Their long boots. Her pink flesh. Steel held in one armpit. Sensing its own imminence, the sow at last kicked out and babbled; the penned pigs began to stamp. But Joachim ignored the uproar. Smiling faintly, he directed the insurance man to smooth the tarp. Then he gave the pig a friendly pat so that, for one moment, it went tranquil. Just long enough for Joachim to sigh and, as Mary breathed—once, twice—to slit the pig's neck from side to side in one long stroke as if there never was another choice.

The pig faded, slow and down in its own blood, draining steadily—it would not stop—its death was programmatic. The rest of the slaughter moved on swiftly. Flipping the dead pig over, Joachim sliced the belly open, and the guts—a ruddy bouillabaise—slid out against his knees. With another cut, he tossed the viscera into separate buckets. Still another: the hooves, the head. Joachim was deliberate about the ways in which life was quartered: he carved each from each as though all bodies one day revealed to him this hidden expectation—each ball and joint, every cell. For Joachim, flesh could be dismantled not unlike the engine of a car.

When Oskar turned again Mary was all eyes, admiring the precise movements of his father's wrists, the follow through with arm and shoulder as he tugged and pulled fat from muscle using all his strength. She could not turn; she didn't want to turn. Mary was in awe of her new knowledge: the body was reducible, it wasn't whole unto itself. As the knife went about its efficient business, and the pig blood puddled on the tarp, Mary looked down, studied their reflections in its shallows. The men laboring with their tools and buckets. At Oskar looking on, one step away. Then—as the sow's blood swelled around her feet—Mary saw her reflection too. The image of a girl.

Letters from H.

To keep from forgetting a wife who died three weeks ago. A wife whose image was already fading from his mind though pictures of her surrounded him. (They were on the mantel, on the wall—there—next to the blue cuckoo clock his mother gave them for their wedding). To keep from forgetting his *mental portrait* of his wife. Not just the shape of her eyes or nose, or the long lines of her neck but, in particular, how she moved. The way she seemed to rustle as she hurried toward the kitchen. Full of puff and shudder—a bird relishing its swallow pride—before she settled at the table or brewed a pot of tea. From fragile brow to lopsided chin. From soft belly to her ankles. All of her stirred and stirring by the same currents in the trees. To keep from forgetting all this and more. How she held his shoulders when he came home from work, pulled him tightly to her in the smooth meat of her hands. Blinking, always blinking, when she looked into his eyes. An excessive blinking, really, that implied a lack of focus. An interruption of the gaze they shared, the gaze he was accustomed to sharing. No doubt it was involuntary since it made her forehead crease. Made the arch of each eyebrow bend in toward the other, angle up and over her nose like two waves erupting into the dark well of an eddy.

To remember *all* of this. To prevent the memory of his now dead wife from fading over time, he decided to write letters—missives to himself from her as though she had written them. Letters he forged in her hand as he often did before she died (a habit of which she was aware), and which he did much more of now (he knew she wouldn't mind). Her letters to him were always short (no doubt because he wrote them). It was a limit he acknowledged even as he penned the letters, even as he mailed them. Even as he read each letter delivered to the box outside his house from which it had been sent.

He was under no illusions the moment he identified the body sealed in plastic at the morgue. Hikers had pulled it from the car before firemen arrived—long before he got the message he was needed by police. How *could* he have illusions as he was escorted to the morgue? As an officer explained to him that, sadly, his wife was dead, that—tragically—his wife had died. That her car was tossed from Elbow Lane as though by a shying horse. *It's really not surprising*, the officer explained to him. *Accidents are common there. After all, the curve is perilous*, his wife must have known the danger. Yet the hikers claimed she'd been driving fast. *Recklessly*, the detective said, as he rocked slowly on his heels. Fault would be withheld, however, until after an investigation. Until the detective looked into why the car skidded and then missed the turn. Why a wife drove her Chevy first through a guard rail. Then into the wall of a granite mausoleum. So that by chance the wife had died inside a cemetery.

The first letter arrived a month after she was gone. A month after he watched the coffin sink into the ground. A coffin sealed even at the wake. His wife's body so disfigured that the cosmetologist balked, recommended a closed coffin. *There is just not enough*, the young woman had explained, appealing to him with her small pink eyes so that she could pack her gauze and rouges and leave the mortuary. There is just not enough. Not nearly enough left of the whole and living wife. The wife gouged and pressed inside a coffin that she herself had made.

The first letter greeted him with her simple *Thomas*. It was a greeting he was used to. A greeting that he'd longed for since she'd stopped writing letters to him a few weeks before she died. She was a letter writer. A writer of words who believed her thoughts had meaning only after they were postmarked. That her words became permanent only once they were severed from their author's hand. That, abandoned by her, words collected meanings to them like the lint she plucked from his suit each evening when he came home from work. Residues she gathered in her palm, then rolled up in a ball, before she tucked them into a sandwich bag, taking pleasure in their slow accretion over the course of several months, much as she delighted in the way her words returned to her, reappeared in their mailbox so that he could read them to her aloud after supper. Even before they married, she entrusted her thoughts to the postal service—

delaying her reply to his marriage proposal just so she could stamp it. Send it through the mail. Then stand by him as he opened it as if she had forgotten what the letter said, or believed that her answer—a "yes" printed in thick red crayon—could have changed once it was postmarked. Even now he saved that note. Stored it in a firebox he bought one year ago in case of a crisis not unlike the crash that killed his wife. He kept the box in the basement: it protected her letters, all her notes of affection, the swift and offhand jottings filled with her concerns. *Impatient thoughts*, she told him, which would never wait for his return from work and so had to be written down. Then aged in the postal system so that, three days later, when her letters arrived back in their box, her thoughts seemed less impetuous. They were mellowed, more composed.

THOMAS—

Even as you read this, I am thinking of you— thinking of you as I write this letter to remind you of the last one that I sent. How strange to be at home without you, to walk through the kitchen and swipe up crumbs from your breakfast toast, leftovers which remind me that just a short time ago you were sitting in this kitchen. But the memory is vague, as though your recent nearness has obscured its clarity. Do you find it odd that I'm still surprised when you return each day? Bring me flowers, something bright, and perhaps I'll press them for us, hang them on the wall. They'll help me to remember that I haven't just

*imagined you, that I have not made up this life which
we share together.*

— H.—

The second letter came with a knock on the door. A knock rapped by the tan knuckles of the postman. The same postman who delivered mail every afternoon. For six years, slipping letters in the mailbox or leaving parcels on the porch. Today, the postman knocked to determine if anyone were home. Whether the resident of 5 Heron Way would accept the parcel he'd brought for him, a small box from a service from which the resident had often purchased automotive gadgets for a Chevy that (by all accounts) no longer needed replacement parts. Or any parts at all. Silently, the resident stepped out on the porch. And the postman laid the parcel on his outstretched palms along with several letters.

The first letter that he opened was a letter from his wife. Or, more precisely, the letter he mailed to himself as though his wife had written him, and which the postman had delivered (pulling the missive from the satchel and setting it on top) as though a postman's duty was not just to deliver mail, but also to arrange it, to organize each letter for him in the order it should be read.

THOMAS—

Just now the blue clock struck noon and when I drew back the curtains, sunlight filled the room. I am sitting inside a ray of light, just a particle—floating—like so many others. In here, we're all bright: I can't even see my hand, the fingers which now hold my pen. No doubt this is a sloppy letter, I'm sorry if it's hard to read: I just wanted to share its warmth with you. But now someone is knocking. The postman is knocking, and I must answer the door.

—H.—

The third letter arrived in the mailbox one week later, on top of a new stack the postman had arranged, sales pamphlets on the bottom, then the monthly bills, and new letters of condolence. Letters of sympathy still filled his box. But, lately, their tone had changed. The letters less interested now in tearful reminiscence than in praising his courage, his capacity for bearing up. For managing so well even though a group of engineers had found a defect in the Chevy's wires. A weakness in the brakeline about which he'd been unaware as he drove the car to and from work, stopping—suddenly—as he often did. It was a dangerous habit, his wife had warned him: he followed cars too closely. *You're tailing them,* she'd say, *and one day you'll pay for it,* careen into the bumper of the car in front *and then what will you do?* He hadn't known, of course, about the Chevy's defect, nor that his driving likely made the problem worse, until the accident six weeks ago when the line finally ruptured as his wife drove around a bend.

A dangerous curve on Elbow Lane with which she should have been familiar since she drove the same route to work each day. To her own shop: a lingerie store that shared its parking lot coincidentally with the local post office.

Her first few days of work, her messages were hasty. Notes scrawled on bank receipts and clothes tags when she perhaps sat down to lunch. And then for two weeks—nothing—no mail at all. Though his wife both promised and swore to him she'd send new letters soon, *in a week perhaps* when her new duties eased. When she became more confident in the business and could spend less time at work.

> THOMAS—
>
> *At last I have time,* she had written on the napkin, *at last I can write to you as I've always done. You must know that I'm worried for you—what have you been dreaming? Why have you been waking up in the middle of the night? Take comfort in me...tell me tonight what's been troubling your sleep.*
> —H.—

He didn't know that she knew about the nightmare. The dream that could always wake him when, while safe in bed, he nonetheless found himself running across a pitch black stage, sidewinding in the darkness. He never told his wife about it. Never confessed to her that he was hunted as soon as he fell asleep. Yet why was he surprised? As he told her many times (even that last morning): she often guessed his needs before he knew them himself. She agreed of course. Cupped his chin. Pulled it close to hers so that their faces appeared together in a mirror across the kitchen—her brown eyes reflecting (as they always did) deceptively rapid feelings, flashes of spite and pleasure which blew through them like battling winds. Her gaze sank into his face, into his flesh. She blinked when he smiled. Once. Then again. Her lepidopteran eyes.

He was surprised, however, when he received her next note. A postcard that for the first time bore him no greeting and which, he suspected, the postman had read: *I know something,* she wrote simply. *I know something you don't want me to know.* The rest of the message had been censored. The words crossed out with marker so that the card itself seemed black. As he tore it, prepared to toss the postcard in the fire, the ink smudged on his fingers. Dyed his skin to match her words.

The fifth letter arrived in the hands of the police, carried by them from his box with all his other mail. The officers arrested him as soon as he opened it—as he unfolded its single sheaf for them all to read. Like the previous note, this one lacked a greeting. It was blank. Nearly blank. There were just a few words printed at the bottom: *Every road takes me back to a past I can't recall,* she wrote. *Where does that leave me now?*

The officers were nice enough to let him take his hat and scarf. The winter wear his wife knit for him before she took her job in town. Before she began to drive to work, speeding (braking) on Elbow Lane so that, as she drove around the bend (as everyone in town now knew), she one day simply *lost control.* Burst through a guard rail, into a wall. The officers were nice enough to let him take her letters with him. In fact, they encouraged him to bring the whole box along. All the notes she'd ever sent to him so that he would not forget her.

He confessed to his wife's murder at six:fourteen that evening. The same time, he told them, that his wife was pronounced dead by firemen who arrived too late. He told detectives how he'd done it: he confirmed their new evidence which suggested his wife's accident wasn't an accident at all. *It's your doing,* the detective said, *we'll find it in the letters. Now fess up. Don't waste our time. We've got better things to do.* They had changed their minds, his lawyer said, after a postman had come forward. After a postman had informed them that the (now dead) wife was fond of mail. Specifically, she was still *sending* mail long after she had died. *If you killed her, tell us now,* the detectives had advised him. Why go on, put up a fight? It was easy: he confessed.

Fourteen days later, the police dropped the charges after a writing expert reviewed the notes, compared the recent letters with the ones stored in the box. This expert, his lawyer told him, had explained to the police that the letters his wife sent *before* her death and the others she sent *after* were in fact penned by the exact same hand. *The husband perhaps re-sent old notes,* the expert had suggested, *in envelopes she wrote before she died.* You see, the lawyer said, *forgery is not so easy. There are subtle nuances to every script, stresses on curves and crosses which reveal a forger's hand. Phrases that expose the way a forger thinks.* His lawyer leaned forward in his chair. *In other words, the expert thinks the letters aren't evidence that any crime occurred.*

Against the advice of his lawyer, he confessed again that evening. *Hire a new expert,* he appealed to the detectives. *Find another expert who will testify I wrote the notes*—then sent them through the mail. That in order to remember *everything about my wife,* he had focused on recalling the inflection of his wife's written voice—the style of her perceptions—so that he could perfect both her script and thoughts. *Nuances,* he explained, which enabled him to write the letters as though his wife had written them. Even to rebuke himself much as his wife once did.

The lawyer applauded the new confession the next day, and everyday thereafter that his client went down to the station to confess his "crime" again. *You're a genius,* the lawyer told him. *The police are confused. If there were any doubts remaining about your innocence, you've wiped them out completely. They think you're mad, struck down by grief.* (His lawyer thumped him on the back.) *They're not searching for new evidence. Rest easy. You're home free.*

The detectives were kind enough to listen to his story at six: fourteen each evening when he went down to the station. Patiently, they'd nod their heads as, once again, he told the tale of how he'd planned to kill his wife. How he pulled it off (it took one year), how difficult it was. After pouring him a coffee, the detectives would once more explain that he could not in fact have killed his wife. That he could not have frayed the brakeline. That their expert proved conclusively that he could not have forged the notes. *The wiring had a tragic flaw, the engineers discovered it. As for the letters, well,* the detective smiled, *she wrote those herself.* The detective then suggested that he *ought to see a therapist,* that *talking to a therapist might help you clear your thoughts,* since the letters seemed to him a "cry for help," though he wasn't an authority. *It's grief which makes you say such things. It's understandable.* The detective stood and brought him his coat. *Now go home,* he said and shook his hand. *We know you're not guilty.*

The Villa of
the Veiled Lady

In August, the sun hovered above the ruins of Herculaneum. The heat was fierce, the earth parched. Only dragonflies swarmed the streets of the city that once was buried in ash. As Alice approached the gates to the site, an old man in a booth waved her over. "We close at five," he said as he sold her a map and a ticket. Then he pointed her down a cobbled street that had ruts worn by wheels in the stones.

Although Alice heard the clatter of hand tools off in the distance where the digging continued, the excavated center of the city was silent. Still, even. She left the main thoroughfare and, having studied the map, followed the side streets to the southeastern corner of town. It was old homes, a dead life, that Alice wanted to see—the broken walls built from paper and dust, spent embers, tiny insects, and sand.

In the long moment of the late afternoon heat, the distance Alice traveled to get to the ruins was of little consequence to her. Where she began was implicit—a green suburb of Philadelphia where they still tip the postmen—but her home, her town and circle of friends, they were no longer *of* her journey. She had left them behind, made an exchange of the past for the present: a past that would likely become her future, for a present that was unknown. For three weeks, she rode the trains, sometimes rented a Vespa, traveled from big toe to ankle, up the calf of the Italian countryside. Perhaps when she arrived in Milan—perhaps then she would go home. For now, just a few things mattered: where she ate dinner, slept for the night, where she would head off to in the morning. There were too many places to trek through, to eat through, to buy tickets to see. For Alice, time seemed scarce. So she'd begun to hoard it. The past couldn't be changed; the future would take care of itself. For now—for the present—Alice would *see* (that was her duty). She wanted to see more than anything else. Her guidebook with its maps, its suggestions, was everything, was precious to her; there was little to do at home.

Alice was, in other words, that new breed of American—part of an over-optioned middle class, full of investment portfolio chatter, although her parents, with whom she still lived, continued to reside in their familiar, split-level home.

Today, Alice was tired, she'd had it. For hours, she walked through the ruins, through homes and temples, baths, ball courts and toilets, even sat for a time on a listing block of seat at the omnitheater. She hadn't seen everything, but she'd seen enough, and the sun, still high and bright—enormous, as it was, over the excavation all day—was fading, not in strength, but against the tick of the clock. Soon, the groundskeepers would call her in, round her up, expel her with the rest of the flaggers out into the streets of the city above the city: the modern day Ercolano which, like a grown child standing over an elderly parent, overlooked the site of the ruins.

Outside the building that archaeologists had named House of the Stags (for the stag sculptures unearthed inside), Alice found a bench and sat on it. She was hot, she needed to rest, and her canteen was filled with stale water. She sipped it anyway, spat in the dust. At first, the dry earth refused to absorb it. But then with an almost perceptible sigh of irritation, the earth seemed to relent. When she looked back a few moments later, the damp sand was already dry.

"Hello?"

Though Alice knew no one, had met no one, knew of no one who might look for her among the ruins, she sat up and looked around.

"Signorina?"

It was the same voice, neither soft nor loud, friendly nor urgent. After a moment, she found it, *him*, hidden among stone gray and shadow in the half-light of the building's portico.

"Me?" Alice said, rubbing her eyes as if to see him more clearly. He was leaning against a column, had propped himself there as comfortably as if the House of Stags were his own home. From just a few feet away, she could smell his cigar. He was sucking on it, letting a perilous tumbler of ash grow at its tip just above a thick kerchief loosely tied at his neck.

He was watching her watch him; he was a patient man. Clearly, he wasn't a tourist.

Alice called out to him again.

"Me?" She pointed to her shirt to emphasize her meaning. It was soaked, she realized, thinking, not for the first time, that the sun and the city were in hostile collusion against the curious visitor—the sun sapping from tourists the fluids the long dead city needed to bring life back to the parched buildings and dusty streets, an urbanity buried in ash. After all, much like its sister city Pompeii which Alice had toured just one day before, Herculaneum had been built beneath an active volcano that, long ago and since again, had erupted with catastrophic force over the cities in its shade. While much of Pompeii had been unearthed, Herculaneum—a small town in comparison—still remained largely concealed. As Alice had read, the pyroclastic blanket which interred the city was as hard as concrete. For diggers, it was tough going. Not only were they hampered by the solid matrix of ash and mud, but by the complaints of the locals in the city above who threw chestnuts, chastized them, whenever a modern building was imploded to make way for the past.

From the doorway, the man at last emerged, his hands turned up as though in supplication. He stopped just a few feet away, rocked back on his heels. At first, she thought he was nervous—there was a peculiar excitement about him. Yet he was all motion without actual movement. There was little plot to him, Alice decided, as she looked him over. He didn't make her uneasy; she didn't feel wary, even though she noticed he wore calfskin pants in the heat.

"Come," he said at last, adding, as though he had carefully chosen his words (or perhaps his translation of them): "I show you something you like."

Turning his back, he walked a few feet away, then looked over his shoulder. He was surprised, Alice realized, that she hadn't followed, that she had remained, feet stretched out before her, resting on the bench.

"Come come," he said, clapping his hands. He was perturbed, there was no other word for it. Alice couldn't help it: she laughed.

"What's your name?" she asked.

He bowed. "In Italian," he said, "they call me Apollinaro. In English, they say Tebel. They are two different names—not the same name in two different tongues. Always, however, my last name is Vos." He could hold a conversation, it seemed, even with half of his tongue wrapped around a cigar.

"My mother, you see, she was English, the people who raised me, from New Ercolano, the city above." He sighed. "The story is complicated and not complicated at all."

"Vos," she said. "That's an English name too?"

"A Welsh name," he said. "My father is not known."

She considered. "What should I call you then?"

"Whatever you like." Again he bowed, not from the waist, but by waving his arm out in an arc around him as though he were wearing a cape.

Alice—reflecting on Romans and being in Rome, at least an ancient Roman city—made her decision without effort. "Apollinaro," she said, "I'm afraid I can't come." She tapped the watch on her wrist. "It's almost time to leave."

Apollinaro stepped toward her, took the cigar from his mouth and put a silencing finger across his lips. "True," he said. "But you see here," he pulled a ring of keys out his pocket. "I have the ways in and out." He sat next to her on the bench. He looked very serious.

"I watch you today," he said. "You like to look at things. Let me show you what they keep hidden here." He took her hand and stood up, pulling her with him. "You will like it," he said. "For you, I make a guarantee." Apollinaro thumped his chest and, knocking some of the ash into his kerchief, cursed, let go of her hand. He swiped at his neck and loose ash was suddenly around them in the air.

Under how much ash had this street once been buried, Alice considered. And now this capful of it rising softly, almost gently, between them.

She looked back at Apollinaro. He was watching her, he'd gone very still. Then, reaching out, he took her hand again in both of his. His grip was damp but tough. If not for the heat, she guessed it would be cool. And there was a strength he had not used.

"OK," Alice said, trying to look him hard in the eye. "But no funny stuff."

"No funny stuff," he agreed. Surprising herself, Alice believed him.

At first they walked slowly away from the House of the Stags toward the edge of the city, away from the forum and baths, the shops and patrician homes, always toward the outskirts, the edge of the excavation and the steep hills of its perimeter which made the old Roman site look, from the city above, as if it had been built in a crater—as though it were a lunar resort spackled together with a mortar of cheese.

Apollinaro wasn't tall but he was taller than Alice, and though at first he picked a pace that suited her stride, he quickly forgot and began to let out his length. Soon she was jogging slowly behind him just to keep up, so she wouldn't lose him among the new digging sites through which they wove—in and out—even the ones that had been blocked off and which, smiling, he led her through so they could swiftly get to the particular site he wanted to show her: a squat but sprawling building in front of which a wheelbarrow and shovels had been left behind. A bucket, some brushes, sat by one doorway, a canteen on its head against a wall. Evidently, the workers had left for the day; not one of them could be seen.

Unconcerned, Apollinaro grabbed her hand and pulled her through the doorway, into the shaded concourse of a massive hall.

"Here," he explained, "a place for many shops." He flourished his arm as if—right at that very moment—he had discovered the building himself.

"An arcade?" Alice asked as she looked round.

He nodded and began to pull her from shop to shop inside the hall, pointing at a jug still filled with grain, at a nearby hearth where a copper pot hung, a thick chain securing it level over an iron grate in the floor. In another shop, they found a loom and a press and the remains of several baskets inside of which corroded bolts of fabric, scorched rope and yarn, still seemed to await purchase. Further inside, a baker's oven and loaves of bread lined up on a shelf for display.

"I said you will like," he smiled as she walked around making soft sounds of pleasure, kicking up dust as she hurried along, bending here and there to get a better view of the grain and the fabric, of how delicately the eruption had encased the arcade and preserved its contents, while other buildings, some nearby, had been stripped, had become nothing more than ember, beam, and tottering stone.

"Amazing," she said and reached out to trace the outline of a fish a long dead baker had drawn into the crust of a loaf on his counter. Quickly Apollinaro grabbed her hand, rapped her fingers with his own.

"Only for looking," he said. "You remember."

Alice nodded and began to pull her hand from his, but he already had released it. Instead, he took her by the arm and led her back outside the marketplace. Around the backside of the building, they tripped over loose dirt and digging equipment, scaffolding not yet erected or already dismantled. At last, he stopped in front of a low window into which he leaned, then pulled himself through. Once he righted himself, he leaned back out and reached for her hand. The window, apparently, was the only entrance into an otherwise sealed off room. Earth and a dense packed mud still blocked a doorway off to her left.

Alice gave him her hand and scrambled in after him. At first, the room was dark, far too dark for her to see as she strained her eyes. But quickly Apollinaro sparked up his lighter, let the flame curl high and bright above the fist he closed tightly around it. Across the room, they walked together until they stood in front of a small pedestal of hard mud which revealed the shape of a crib, a cradle perhaps. As Apollinaro leaned over it, Alice followed the path of the flame. Inside, there was a pile of tiny bones, the ashen outline of an infant. The baby must have been carbonized, completely burnt by the molten mud which once had filled the room. How strange that other bodies had been preserved, soldiers and citizens, even pets, choked by the burning ash, the gases, which rained down in the streets, their bodies later wrapped in a blanket of pumice and mud so that, centuries later, their pain didn't seem spent: the bones still clutched hair and clawed at the ground, tore at eyes in disbelief.

Yet this infant had been reduced to nothing more than a trace in its bed, an outline perhaps of what could have been: a mark for the future of a long dead past which only had meaning—right then at that moment—when Alice stood over it and looked down.

"Let's go," she said suddenly shaken. He nodded, and it seemed to Alice as he gave her his hand, helped her back out through the window, that, much like her, Apollinaro let out a sigh of relief.

Her guide was quiet as they returned to the path toward the perimeter of the ruins. And though he stuffed his hands in his pockets, let the cigar seem to breathe for him as the air around Alice choked with its haze, he looked surprisingly stern in his outrageous getup. For a moment, she could see the Brit in him, the imprint of the mother beneath his more Mediterranean nature. At last he said, "My friend, there are no more bones in that house."

Alice wasn't sure what he meant, but presently it came to her.

"You think the child was left behind?"

Apollinaro nodded. And Alice fell silent too.

After a time, the path they walked on began to sway up hill, a steady grade toward the banks of the perimeter. It was a gentle rise at first, but when she looked back at the excavation behind them—now, in fact, below them—she realized just how far they'd climbed. It was a graveyard he'd brought her to. Around them, the tops of columns rose from the ground like footstools. The tips of rooftops marked the burial place of homes still hidden below, perhaps with their owners inside.

Beyond, steep walls encircled the ruins. Above, the highrise slums of New Ercolano perched on the edge of the crater. They were scheduled for demolition, Apollinaro explained. But Alice could still see laundry pinned to lines between the tenements; the residents had not yet moved.

Apollinaro guided her toward a large structure whose topmost floor had been hollowed out of earth, though the bottom levels—a first and second floor—clearly were still buried. The building was surrounded by iron pikes through which a thick blue rope was strung. Warning signs hung from it cautioning curious wanderers from entry.

Apollinaro spat a bit of cigar on the ground.

"Not to worry you," he said, dismissing the signs. "Only for the babies." With that, he slid through a window much like before, stamping his feet inside the room to reassure Alice as she waited outside that the ancient floor was safe.

"Come come," he called to her. "This house is special." He extended his hand through the window, knocked a stone from the crumbling sill that skittered to Alice's feet. "Good girl," he said when she took his hand anyway and climbed onto the ledge. But before she could jump down next to him, he put a hand on her knee, stopped her from moving. "Wait," he said. "Give me the feet." Alice was perplexed. "Come come," he said again. Awkwardly, she swung around so that she could sit on the sill with her feet dangling toward him.

"No funny stuff hey," he comforted her as he started removing her shoes. "I put the shoes right here. Next to mine, you see?" He pointed at the pairs of shoes he lined up neatly and smiled. "We leave no traces, we walk gently, we must."

Then he winked and she tried to smile, but for the first time she felt cautious, inexplicably nervous.

"You feel it too?" he said seeing her face curl up. "You are not the first. The diggers, they feel the same way in this house. No one is knowing why." He shrugged. "This house, they think it will fall." (He patted her hand when she stepped back in surprise.) "It is good *now*," he assured her. "Later, when they must do more digging, there is the problem. For now," he said, "it is like rock." He stamped his feet. It was true, the room felt like a cave, sturdy, reliable, with the smell of wet, old stone and dead things that have become dust.

Apollinaro sighed. "Later, when they begin to dig, they will build this house again stone by stone. But it's never the same, I see it over and over. It's the same house with the same parts, but never the same house again." He looked at her. "The feeling you feel when you come in this house, the feeling even *you* had, that will be gone. The house is gone, and all that's left are its stones." He took a deep breath, ran his hand on the air as if touching a fresco revealed there. "It is never like this again," he said smiling sadly. "A one-time opportunity, eh?"

Alice smiled back, and took the hand that he offered. He seemed to take pleasure simply from being a guide. How lucky she'd been to get in his way.

"A one-time opportunity," she agreed nodding seriously as he helped her down from the sill.

The room into which they climbed was an anteroom, a small cubicle off a much larger one which itself led out to the open air—onto a covered terrace supported by columns off which many other rooms had likewise been built on a rectangular plan. Each room had a view of the city and also overlooked an internal garden. An atrium perhaps. Alice only could guess.

On the wall of the larger room, frescoes had been preserved largely intact, though a large corner section had disappeared as if it were peeled away. At its center, there was a woman. She was wearing white—a diaphanous gown that suggested the curves of her breasts, her belly, beneath it. There was a veil over her face, a drapery made of the same fabric so that there was only the hint of dark hair loose to the shoulder, a strong nose, dark eyes staring out. Alice sensed that the veiled lady wasn't smiling beneath all the fabric. Yet she wasn't unhappy—it seemed, rather, as if she were patiently waiting. The veiled lady had waited for many things, Alice guessed, not just the artisan who portrayed her with care to finish the work over which he clearly had labored. The veil and the gown fell to her ankles. Just above the hem, however, there was a pair of lovely, bare feet, their pink toes pointing out as though her body weighed lightly on them.

"She is in every room," Apollinaro said softly. "In each room painted different, but painted the same."

"She's beautiful," Alice said.

"Come come." Her guide took her hand, and pulled her out to the terrace, and slowly they began to walk through the rooms. In the next one, the veiled lady was sitting and washing her feet, her gown bunched up at her knees, so that the lower part of her calves were also revealed. In the room beyond that, she was resting on one hip on a pillow as she played a Roman game of knucklebones. Again she was covered, only her feet could be seen, but this time there was also one delicate hand, the fingers curled back to reveal the knucklebone pieces she'd shaken like dice in her palm. In the next fresco, she was resting, one arm thrown back and under her head, her knees bent, feet pointing away from the painter. In another, she quietly looked off through a window. Elsewhere, she poured wine in a cup. Each painting was different, but Apollinaro was right. They were the same. It was the same woman, wearing the same opaque veils. In each painting, her face was concealed, but she always looked back at the painter, directly out of the fresco at the people who saw her. She was staring out at her life as though through a mirror. As if the ruins were the fresco, charred rock, the still life. As though she still had a presence, a life of her own, if not life as such.

"Who is she?" Alice asked Apollinaro, her hand on his arm as they both studied the frescoes.

"No one knows," he said. "But the diggers, they call her Antonia."

"I feel like she's watching me."

Apollinaro patted her hand. "Yes," he said simply. That was all.

Taking Alice's hand in his, he led her next to a corner room which, unlike the others, had been badly damaged by flows of mud. The tile had buckled in waves, and one wall sloped toward them as though a giant had leaned against it until the mortar and stone gave beneath the weight. Through a window the sun shined in. There were no frescoes on the walls.

"Oh my," Alice said.

On the floor of the room, an outline of a body had been drawn in chalk over the roll and buckle of tile. The chalk itself had been left in the corner, tossed aside and forgotten.

Apollinaro came to a halt. "I was not thinking," he said. "I could not know it still was here."

"What happened?" she asked.

"A sad story."

She urged him on. "Please tell me."

"One month ago," he began, "the diggers came here to work. Instead they found their friend there on the floor, the *carabinieri*, the police, standing over his body, while a woman—a woman who was not his wife—wept in the corner. There was an investigation. It was the police who made the chalk picture. But what was to prove when all was to see? The digger's heart simply gave out. So the wife found out about the young woman, her dead husband. Both of them all in one day."

"How awful." Alice shook her head.

"The girl's name was Antonia," he said. "So the diggers, they named the veiled lady for her. You see, the day that he died, the girl had a look: angry and sad at the same time." Apollinaro shook his head. "That's how the diggers think the veiled lady's face must be under all her veils. Why else would a painter hide her face? They think it is too sorrowful to see."

Alice nodded (she could think of nothing to say), and Apollinaro slowly walked out of the room, left her alone over the chalk drawing of a man—a stout man it seemed—who had curled up on his side, thrown one arm out as he died. The other must have been over his chest, over his heart when it failed.

After a time, Alice followed her guide, found him next door by the painting that portrayed the veiled lady asleep. Apollinaro was standing very still in front of it, his hands out as if he could lift the veil, peel back a layer of paint, reveal her face at last. Still breathing the dusty cigar and sweating in his calfskin pants, he looked large and sad, though Alice couldn't say why. It wasn't from loss, she slowly decided, there was more. Perhaps the inconceivability of losing.

"She means something to you," Alice said after a time, after he'd closed his face down, let the warm emotion retreat when he felt her join him in the room.

He didn't answer her directly. "Do you think she looks like the diggers say? Full of sorrow under her veils?"

Alice thought for a moment. "When I first saw her," she told him, "I thought she simply looked patient, as though she were waiting, but for what I couldn't say. I think she's watching us, though, not hiding from our view."

Apollinaro turned and took her hand. "Just so," he said squeezing it. Then he sighed. "But the diggers, they tend to be stubborn, you can't change their minds once they have been set. They know stone," he went on, "and so like stone they are." He smiled, rapped his skull lightly with his fist. Alice laughed because he wanted her to. Though she didn't think he believed what he said.

"You're not a digger yourself, then?"

"No," he said. "The man who raised me, he still works here even though he is too old. The men let him come and sit on the rocks, use the small brushes to clean up pieces that won't be damaged if he drops them."

"How kind," she said.

Apollinaro grunted. "If he stays home, he just gets older. It is much better this way."

Alice laughed softly and he smiled.

"You are very nice for an American," he said.

"And you," she said taking his arm as though she'd known him much longer than just an hour, "are fortunate to be more Italian than Brit."

He smiled but looked sad and, unexpectedly, Alice felt very small.

"I'm sorry," she said. "I didn't intend to be mean."

Apollinaro pushed at her shoulder gently. "No worries," he said. "You are probably right." He looked back at the painting. And together they fell into the ancient silence that protected the ruins, its stale air of ash and earth, of the paint that had crumbled off the old walls where insects fed in the dark. The veiled lady had looked over it all, silent, unseen and always alone. Alice felt a sudden immanence—of herself and the lady there in the room, of Apollinaro standing beside her and, not so far away, the room where the digger had died, where his woman had cried over him in the dirt. Alice went very still and closed her eyes trying to make them all align as if they were a single point in her mind—a point of time within the time of the ruins, because, at that moment, as she stood in the villa with Apollinaro beside her wearing leather and ash, she felt as though she might be able to feel it, feel time itself or at least sense its shape—where she was *in time*, and where Apollinaro and the veiled lady were, not so far away, in relation to her in time's scheme.

"She seems so familiar," Alice said slowly, carefully, watching his reaction. "Like a woman we'd each like to know at some point in our lives."

For the first time, Apollinaro studied her not as a guest, but like a man with a past, a history guarded by custom. He looked fierce as he dug his toe in the dirt and, suddenly, Alice was sad that she had broken the air with her voice. It was a rare thing to feel silence lap at one's body like warm water over a stone.

Her curiosity—her desire to know the rest of his story—was presupposed, she realized. He assumed she would try to pry his memories, his feelings, from him simply because they were part of her own adventure. And he was right. It was the American in her, Alice decided, and she tried to let it go, let the silence fill her again, fill them both like empty patterns in the dust. All around her, she thought, the stones, the villa and its veiled lady too: they were ancient, and they were the same. She and the veiled lady and Apollinaro standing right by her. They were ancient and new; they were the same. It was just a matter of perspective, she thought. Of seeing it all together against the same shape, of making the shape *fit* one's perspective.

There was a certainty Alice often sensed, but which came over her at inconvenient times. When, for instance, she walked by an old man on the sidewalk bending toward his destination, stuttering from one shoe to the next without any help, without even the hope of support. It was the same feeling she had when she sat near a woman eating her supper alone: that a small gesture could be everything—that an offered arm, a word spoken simply, could be everything in itself. Of course she'd never done much about it, never given her arm or said the word; there was always some place to be, some future to make. And she lived, after all, in a city.

"Wait here," she said to her guide, moving before she could stop.

She returned quickly to the corner room where the digger had died. In the west, the sun was setting beyond the horizon of the two cities, the one new, the other old, though they both bore the same name. The sun was retrieving its last stiff rays from the window, recoiling its light from the leftover chalk she'd seen cast off to the side. Quickly, she picked it up. When she returned, Apollinaro was still standing with his hands in his pockets looking up at the woman in veils.

"Lay down," she told him.

"Scusi?" he said.

"Trust me," she said. "Lay down."

Perplexed, Apollinaro squatted down on his haunches, then rolled onto his back with a soft grunt. He rested his head on the back of one arm, put the cigar in his mouth, and, looking up, blew a smoke circle which rose up around her as she bent over him and looked down.

"Now what?" he said.

"Hush," she said, then kicked at his boots to make him spread his legs apart. Instead, he just squinted and puffed. "Come come," she said clapping her hands much as he had not long ago, and sighing he did as she asked.

Alice bent down at his side and pressed the chalk hard in the dirt. Slowly, she drew a line around him: down his side, around his heel, up his leg and, quickly, from one thigh to the next, down again then up to his hip, following the flare of his torso into the pit of his arm and around the point of the elbow he had thrust out behind him. Along the curve of his head, she continued to draw, taking into account the curls of his hair, the brief length of neck and the knot of kerchief around it—around and down until line met line and the chalk shape completely enclosed him. Alice stood over Apollinaro and looked at her picture of him: how the two overlapped. Not bad, she thought, and gave him her hand so that when he stood, he wouldn't mess up her work.

Carefully, he got up and stepped out of the image as though he had cut himself from the earth. He walked around it, encircled his image with another pattern of feet. Then stepped back, looked at the two together—at the painting of the veiled lady, and the chalk image Alice had drawn in the dirt—the one on the wall, the other in earth, the two figures waiting together.

"Do you like it?" she asked.

He smiled. "You think it will bring me luck?"

"Yes." She had no doubt.

Quietly, he accepted her gift. Forgave her as he bent and kissed the warm air above her knuckles just as, not a moment before, he had touched the fresco of the veiled lady without touching it at all.

"Thank you," he said softly and looked at her, then beyond her at the light retreating from the hall. Glancing down at his watch, Apollinaro stepped quickly from the room.

"It is late," he said returning, and gestured for her to follow. "The sun has set. We must go now before the darkness." There was urgency in his voice.

Alice stood quickly, and he pulled her from the room, back to their shoes, then over the sill and out of the window. She kept up with him as they loped down the hill and toward the center of the excavation. She kept up even as the light went gray—as the ruins and the sky became the same—and she lost all sense of the horizon. Past the House of the Papyri and the House of the Gem they ran together, past the forum and baths and the marketplace. They ran from the dark which, like a slow rain of ash, began to obscure the light as if it wanted to trap them. Perhaps turn them to stone. Add new citizens to a dead city. They were sweating when they arrived at the gates, as even the last streaks of gray disappeared from the sky as they only can do over the Mediterranean Sea—with a sudden exasperation.

"Good," he said. "We are safe."

He was dusty, she noticed, as he pulled out his keys. His shoes, his pants, even his hair—all of him covered in the fine loose sand that swept through the ruins. Yet his sweat still smelled like ash.

"When do you go home?" he asked. The road outside was cross-hatched by tread marks where rental cars driven by tourists had skidded and come to a halt. While in the darkness behind them, Alice imagined she could still see the Villa off in the distance. The veiled lady was still waiting for them: she would continue to wait for them inside.

"I'll be going soon," she said as she took his hand.

Quietly, he unlocked the gates and they walked into the street that led up to the city above. She could hear music and cars above the dead patience behind them.

It sounded, she thought, like the moon.

Amelia Earhart's
Last Transmission

I was twelve the day my mother vanished while standing at the kitchen sink.

There was a pop! Then she was gone.

I never saw her again.

Let me relate in all simplicity the events that occurred that final day. I know of no other way to describe them.

There we were in the kitchen. My father, as usual, hunched at the table over a pile of toast. Bobby, his mouth full, in front of the refrigerator; while at his feet, our baby sister mashed whatever Bobby dropped—a clot of cheese, tomato pulp— with the soft meal of her hands. Meanwhile, across from them, at the far side of the kitchen, my mother washed the breakfast dishes: already, there was a careful stack of plates draining at her side. I have to admit I was late to the kitchen that morning. My mother had discovered all the bagged lunches I'd stashed in the back of my closet—along with the army of ants that lived there.

"Be quick, Jack," she said sending me off with a garbage bag and a dustpan.

Those were the last words I ever heard her say.

Today, thirty years later, I can still remember how my mother smelled that morning—the way the stale scent of sour milk and Vaseline hung heavy around her in the air. I can clearly recall the humidity of her bathrobe, even the resinous bouquet of her gray-flecked skin as she pressed her wrist against her brow.

Still, my wife, Madeline, claims it's the "idea" of the smell that I really remember. "Not your mother's scent itself." Madeline then adjusts the tinted glasses she usually wears when she meets patients. Until recently, I'd never seen her wear them at home.

I suppose it's not uncommon for a husband and wife to square off at times about their memories. Yet this lone dispute has, over the course of our three year marriage, transformed from the initial commiseration that marked our awkward first meetings whenever I mentioned my mother (who coincidentally shares my wife's name) into frequent and, I might add, uncomfortable inquiries at inopportune times (my wife likes to interrogate me while I'm immersed in the bath) that have devolved into a bitter debate which, given the history of the issue at hand, cannot be worked out. As the sole practitioner of the Pragmatist School of Objective Psychotherapy in our small suburb outside Buffalo, my wife has decided to make my memory the subject of her research. And though I've made my feelings on the matter clear, she is incapable, I'm loathe to say, of simply letting the issue drop. Her career depends on it, she tells me. My answer—that our marriage does as well—has been met with no response. Of course, as everyone in this town well knows, I remain eternally devoted to her. Yet my home life now has become a "situation." Not a place of rest.

In our more peaceful moments, we claim to disagree on

principle and Madeline has even told me that she's recorded my objections to her research among the many footnotes that support her study. Yet, when I recently concluded that she could be right—that her thesis, "Interpretive Variants of Tropistic Scent Recollection," might in fact have some merit—I didn't fess up and tell her. I didn't sit her down and admit at once that, when our son was born six months ago, I noticed she began to secrete a sour smell much like the scent I still associate with my mother: that if I closed my eyes when my wife was near, it seemed, suddenly, that my mother was too. If I'm honest, then, it's quite possible that the distinct smell I recall so clearly from that traumatic day so long ago may in fact represent nothing more than the fortuitous association of several familiar odors—boiled egg and talc for instance—by which all mothers are in some way bound. Of course, I very much want to tell my wife about my recent findings. I can imagine her pleasure at my breakthrough. Even the subsequent applause her research would receive. Yet if I were to admit to her that I now doubt the veracity of my mother's scent, I fear Madeline would go still further: that my wife would go on to claim that my mother couldn't have disappeared—that my entire memory is simply wrong. Unfortunately, I can't explain my (no doubt) baseless fears to my wife. Lately (and I use this word loosely), we haven't seen eye to eye on such matters at all.

But I'm getting ahead of myself when I'd like to tell this story in the proper order, as I suspect my wife and my mother both would have preferred. They were altogether sensible women.

At my new therapist's suggestion, then, I've written down what I remember of my mother's disappearance in a small, leather journal I now keep by my bed. Dr. Sheila—the intern my wife was grooming to help run her practice—claims that it could shed light on what happened in my parents' home thirty years ago, inasmuch as my own home last month.

"So you didn't *see* Madeline leave with quite the same plainness as your mother," Sheila says, pushing her long brown hair behind one ear. "Yet both women are gone all the same. Don't you think it's important to consider the role that untimely absences have played in your life to keep them from occurring again?" She smiles in her winsome way and I find I can't disagree.

Sheila, I should note, claims to believe my story, though I suspect she has more reservations than she's let on. Naturally, that troubles me, and though I've said as much to her, she merely smiles as if she believes she knows my mind better than I do myself. Perhaps it's her easy courage—her conviction that she'll sort me out—that's charmed me lately because, without question, I've done all that she's asked. I've quit drinking and started yoga. I've cut my hair and now take naps. I've even agreed to her gentle request to write a few words in my journal about my sister, Anne—a topic my wife had always avoided herself because, at one time, she was Anne's doctor. In fact, I met Madeline four years ago at Chautauqua Psychiatric as I was visiting Anne. When I signed in, it was Madeline who, clipboard in hand, escorted me to the observation room with its straight-backed chair and one-way mirror. Shortly after, we went out on our first date. At the time, I was a realtor. And Madeline was looking for a home.

Sheila has reviewed my sister's case so she's aware that Anne's condition hasn't changed since the accident fifteen years ago that killed my father and brother as my family was driving to collect me from college. Anne's diagnosis, however, remains merely a vague body of loosely related conjectures. My sister, after all, inexplicably survived the accident without a scratch. Yet, the trauma of my father's death evidently damaged her beyond repair and my then ten year old sister completely regressed into the baby she'd been the day my mother went missing. Since the accident, Anne hasn't spoken a word. She's never left the institution in which she was placed. And because her doctors—even Madeline—claimed that my visits unduly upset her, I stopped seeing Anne a long time ago. It's not that I don't care for my sister. In fact, a book she gave me on my sixteenth birthday—a biography about Amelia Earhart—remained, until recently, one of my prized possessions.

Sheila suggested I make a note of that in my journal as well.

What follows is, at Sheila's request, my best recollection of what happened that day thirty years ago when my mother vanished from our lives.

As I recall, I was the last person to arrive in the kitchen that morning. There was nothing unusual about my tardiness. I was as often late as my brother was prompt. He liked to eat, I liked to sleep—and the chore my mother gave me to clean out my closet didn't set me back: it just gave me a reason for lagging behind. Back then, I never really thought about my family's habits. It merely seemed to me that we had a breakfast routine and we kept to it. Or so I'd always thought.

Yet, as I walked down the short hall to the kitchen that morning, didn't I know something odd was about to happen? That, from the look in my mother's eyes when our gazes locked and she slowly took in my bare feet, the trash dribbling from a hole in the bag tucked under my arm, that my family was on the brink of a transformation that I understand as little now as I did the day we changed? It's true that prior to that morning my mother had often threatened to disappear in just such a fashion. "Bobby," my mother would often shout at my brother, "if you don't pipe down, I'll just ex-*plode*!" or "Jack, I'll just ex-*plode* if you don't clean your room!" Which is to say, I remember being surprised that, when she went, she didn't go big. Didn't supernova right there in the kitchen, take us all out with her, so that we'd at least continue to be the family she'd made—remain together—if in an altered state.

Instead, she kept it simple. Poof! Softly. Perhaps even naïvely. Poof! My mother was gone.

Neither Bobby nor my father noticed.

"Bobby," I whispered.

He turned with a spoon in his hand. There was peanut butter streaked on his face and shirt. He'd been licking the rim of the jar.

"Did you see that?" I pointed to the sink where my mother once stood. Already, the baby—looking for her—had crawled to the place where my mother last was standing. But finding instead only a slick soap bubble residue, Anne had begun to roll herself in it like a shoat trying to recapture its mother's scent after she's left the pen.

"Mom exploded," I explained.

It was apparent Bobby didn't understand.

"What do you mean?" It was an honest question.

"She was standing right there," I said, "when I walked in. And then she wasn't there anymore."

He turned toward the sink and scratched his chin. "Just like she always said she would?"

I nodded.

"How about that," he said (he looked impressed) and he turned and shook my father because I was too stunned to tell him myself. To this day, I read very little into my initial aversion for movement, into my reluctance to dial 911: I was just a boy after all. And though I neglected even to suggest a search for my mother in case my eyes had deceived me, I was clearly in shock. I'd seen something no boy should ever see. Indeed, as far as I know, I remain the only one.

"Dad." Bobby shook my father again when he didn't look up from the morning paper. At that time, my father had an impressive facility for concentration and, immersed in the morning news, he was studiedly ignoring us. I find I now do the same thing when my own son cries for no other reason than to hear his sudden and new infant voice.

Finally, my father looked up.

"Mom exploded," Bobby said.

My father looked toward the sink where she'd been standing a moment before, washing the dishes, stacking them in the drain.

He ignored my brother and turned to me. It was often the way in our family.

"Where is she?" he asked.

"She was standing right there—there," I pointed to where Anne sat cooing and splashing in the light soapy residue all around her, "and then she simply went—poof!—just like that," (I remember I was breathing hard), "and then she was just—*gone*."

I could see he doubted me, though he also realized I wasn't putting him on. It was the same look he'd once given me when, while we were hiking, I gashed my leg and, to his hurried question "where did you get hurt?," I responded by pointing to the rock that tripped me up, rather than the deep wound in my shin.

Just like then, he held his tongue. Waiting to see what might come next.

We could all see that the baby's clothes had grown damp and my father made an abortive effort to reach for her, to rise from his chair and cross the worn linoleum. But when my mother did not appear at once to gather Anne up in her arms, he sat back down with a sigh.

"How about that," he said. He looked as stumped as the rest of us. I remember thinking that, if the three of us looked so much alike at that moment, I must have suddenly grown up.

The baby was making a faint gurgling sound as she clapped her hands and, noting that she was drooling a fine thread of spittle into my mother's remains, I wondered if I ought to sponge up what was left of my parent before Anne inevitably contaminated my mother's final syrupy traces with another kind of mess altogether.

Bobby, meanwhile, was wrapping his sandwich in plastic

(we were late for school). He didn't seem worried and, at that moment, his indifference was a great source of comfort. It was clear he thought she'd be back.

"Has Mom ever exploded before?" Bobby asked, packing the sandwich and several cookies into a paper bag, then stuffing the bag inside his shirt. He'd done the same thing every morning since starting the year at P.S. 99. It left his arms free, he said, if he had to run. Like me, he was often bullied. Unlike me, he was rarely caught.

My father thought for a moment.

"Once."

He thought some more.

"Just after you were born. But she came back a few days later, right in the same spot, as if she'd never left."

Bobby nodded, then looked at the sink. "Maybe we should wait for her here then."

He just wanted to play hooky. I knew it, I'm sure my father did too. But the logic seemed sound to us all.

"Good idea," I added. Really, what else could we do?

My father nodded, and then cleared his throat.

"Right." He pushed his chair back from the table. "Pick up the baby," he ordered. Then: "I'll make breakfast."

We didn't trouble to tell him that there was a plate of biscuits and jam on the counter behind him because, already, he was cooking up a hot meal of eggs, bacon, and blueberry pancakes—and, back then, Bobby was always hungry. So he cooked and we ate. And though no one washed dishes, I did change the baby. Then, later, while my father slept at the table, his head in his hands, Bobby and I turned on the small T.V. that my mother often watched while she cooked. No one answered the phone.

By dinner time, when she hadn't returned, I think we all knew she wasn't coming back. Though we weren't willing yet to admit it.

"How about that," my father said standing by the sink running his fingers through the clear film that, by then, Anne had trailed around the room. There were pieces of banana stuck in it now, sand that Bobby had tracked in with his shoes and, since I'd never dumped the garbage from my room, a small army of ants had escaped the plastic bag and had found, in my mother's remains, a new source of nutrition. They were busily carting her off to their home: I remember thinking that perhaps she'd be happier there.

And so we waited. We sat in the kitchen for days waiting for my mother's return: she deserved that much. But, three days later, when she had not come home, my father rose from the table.

"You've got to go to school," he said.

We nodded: it was true and, anyhow, we'd grown bored. The novelty of my mother's disappearance had worn off. We were sad. But we'd also grown tired. And the baby had a rash.

"Waiting," my father explained, "won't bring her back. And she'd want you to keep up your grades."

We nodded solemnly and ran from the room. And though he and my brother kept a vigil again in the kitchen that evening (and for several evenings after that), I refused to join them. To this day, I still have an aversion to kitchens—though, as Madeline has noted in her study, it's true I'm drawn to loiter outside them, waiting, as my mother once often did, in the displaced air of their doorways, weightless between what my wife describes as a "dwelling's public living space" and the "private heart of every home." I've tried not to read too much into her artless taxonomy. In fact, in the months before my wife also vanished, I tried to read very little into what she said at all: it had become too difficult to figure out what Madeline meant—what I might otherwise describe as her "insinuations"—when she continued to hide behind her tinted glasses. I said as much to her directly of course. I even asked her to take them off.

"Don't be ridiculous," she said. It was not an uncommon response.

Six weeks have gone by since then, and as far as I now can tell Madeline was never truly interested in the precision of my memory, or even how it is that I have such a keen sense of smell. As she often explained, the "char effect" on memory is a thoroughly documented and even "normal" response to complications associated with trauma. Smell channels memory, she said, then interpretation arises. So if a good therapist can identify a scent precisely, the memory associated with it will lay itself bare, like an exposed choke beneath a frond of petals. I'd always thought that was Madeline's object: to peel my mind back as though it were a copse of fierce vegetation. If so, she didn't succeed.

Whatever her motives, Madeline was an ambitious psychotherapist: the notebooks I've paged through since she vanished have done nothing to disprove that. Yet I have to admit that I was surprised to discover that though I thought she was taking notes about my peculiar history, her journals were instead filled with phrases whose meanings I still can't decipher such as "phantom syntax hood," and "steely bob," and even "glottal stop penetration": a code that clearly has nothing to do with me. I've since shown the books to Sheila on the off chance that Madeline's code might represent the jargon of their shared science. Agitated, she flipped through them, then informed me that, regrettably, she couldn't read Madeline's penmanship. It's suspicious: I'm sure Sheila knows more than she'll admit.

Since then, I have come to believe that my wife's research was less about me than her own inevitable disappearance. I'm sure she didn't realize it. Madeline would be the first to say that we're often so bound up by affairs of the past that we fail to correctly interpret the present.

I've tried to question Sheila about it. For a time, she and my wife were close.

"Did you know Madeline was leaving me?" I recently asked her.

Something like a wince crossed her face as we sat side by side on the sofa. But she relented, perhaps because of the look in my eyes—or was it the baby's eyes as I rocked him to sleep?—though I didn't expect what she said.

"Were you aware," she said softly, "that Madeline drove down to Chautauqua shortly before she disappeared?"

I'm sure I frowned. Madeline had no reason to go visit my sister.

"What do you know?" I tried to sound nonplussed.

Sheila looked uncomfortable. It was a conflict of interest to describe my sister's status: Anne, after all, was Madeline's patient. Not hers.

There was a long pause, then she said simply: "Madeline claimed that Anne wrote to her, that Anne asked her to come."

That was impossible of course. Anne hadn't spoken in fifteen years, as Sheila well knew. If Anne had, her doctor certainly would have called me at once. To this, Sheila just shrugged as if she knew nothing more.

I suppose that I'm lucky that my own child—John Robert, we named him, after my father and brother—is too young to have a memory that will one day haunt him. That, unlike me, when he gets older, he won't remember the faint aroma of dried mustard that rose off his mother's skin in the morning like dew evaporating in the first warmth of the sun. Of the two of us—abandoned both—he is clearly the more fortunate. It is not uncommon for parents to feel envy for their children's youth, for the lives they have ahead of them. But what about our jealousy for their short-lived ability to forget?

From what Madeline once hinted to me, I gather that she would have preferred me a similar amnesiac. It has even since occurred to me that her recent disappearance might be nothing more than a ruse, a new phase in her continuing research. So, while I still believe that Madeline will one day return to us, a bound manuscript clutched in one hand, Sheila is right about one thing: this second disappearance has changed me as irrevocably as the first. People go missing, as easily as small objects do—evidently it isn't so unusual—and, "for what it's worth," I've told her, "I don't wonder anymore where lost socks go. I won't search for misplaced keys. I've even given Anne's biography of Amelia Earhart away."

Unfortunately, Sheila doesn't regard my new mindset as progress.

"Jack," she said, burping the baby as we sat on my sofa, though her large brown eyes stayed trained on me. "Do you believe all women disappear?"

After a moment, I took my son from her arms. There was no need for my response—and a few minutes later, she left.

The next morning, I drove down to Chautauqua. Were there any new developments, I asked Anne's doctor as we watched my sister through the one-way mirror in the observation room. He was bored by the question. There hadn't been developments *in years*, he stressed. My sister, after all, was "clinical."

He tapped the mirror. Anne didn't move.

"How many times," he said, "have you been told that?"

"I'd like to show her the baby," I said. It wasn't true. He probably knew that. But he couldn't disagree.

I hadn't passed through the observation room in fifteen years, and so, for a moment, as I walked through the doorway, it felt as though I hadn't just stepped from one room into another, but moved through the mirror itself. That I wasn't visiting my sister, so much as stepping into another life.

I was of course prepared for the changes in Anne's appearance: through the mirror, I'd observed her slow transformation from an active girl to an idle, middle-aged woman over the span of several years. Not only had her figure, for instance, taken on the same amorphous quality of the overstuffed chair in which she spent the day staring out of the window, but her skin, like her hair, had become dry and gray.

It wasn't too much to say that, though she was in fact ten years my junior, Anne now looked even older than me. Yet as I sat down just inches from her, these expected changes seemed, for the first time, oddly familiar. I couldn't place it at first, but as Anne stared at Johnny, and I stared at her, I began to perceive a soft doughy emanation rising from my sister's skin. It was a warm scent and once surely had been full of promise, but now, like fermenting yeast, it had turned sour as it dried. Anne smiled gently at the baby and I realized with a start just how much my sister had come to look like my mother. They shared the same round face, the same sad eyes. Even the small dimple on Anne's soft chin mirrored a scar my mother once had on hers. Yet there was more to it than a simple familial resemblance. Anne had achieved my mother's silent stillness, as if no longer convinced of her own existence, she had learned to draw on the warmth of the people around her, to echo their vitality without giving off any, much as an artificial fireplace will seem from afar to radiate heat, until you draw close and try to warm your hands.

We sat together for some time. The baby, Anne's doctor was pleased to note, seemed to calm her, so he retreated to the far side of the room, leaving my son and my sister to stare at each other with the same wide gaze, share a language of soft grunts and whistles in which I could not participate. I waited. Anne, however, seemed the same as she'd always been. I was disappointed, I'll admit as much. So, when I finally rose to leave and turned to dress the baby in his wool coat and cap, it must have been just a fancy that made me think I heard Anne speak.

"She is on you," I thought I heard her whisper softly, "but cannot see you..."

I turned quickly but, as before, Anne was placidly watching the baby. Yet the reference, familiar to me, was one only she knew that I'd recognize. It was Amelia Earhart's last transmission to the coast guard cutter, Itasca, as Earhart circled, looking for help, just before she disappeared.

"KHAQQ calling Itasca," Earhart had signaled. "We must be on you but cannot see you...gas is running low..."

Earhart was never heard from again.

"Anne?" I said and touched her shoulder. Immediately she began to weep, as she always had during my visits before, and with a look of reproach, her doctor led her away at once.

Since I returned from Chatauqua, it's just been Johnny and I in this big house I once called home. He's a docile baby, and he seems to enjoy resting in my arms as we wander through the house each day, sleeping and eating together in fits and starts as if we share the same uneasy infant schedule. Like his mother, he smells like a soft foreign cheese pressed in wax for safe-keeping. I try to keep him close.

Madeline is coming back—I'm still convinced of that—though Sheila has counseled otherwise. Madeline's clothes are here, so is her checkbook. Even her ring of keys. Items, so I've told Sheila, that suggest my wife intends a swift return.

Shortly thereafter, Sheila and I discontinued our sessions. Not much longer after that, she moved away from Buffalo for good.

In the meantime, waiting keeps me busy. There's a lot to do: I have a son to raise, a house to manage. Madeline's research to complete. There is, after all, her disappearance now to document, and I've taken to adding an entry to this account each day, updating her early notes with a new code of my own. After all, according to my father, my mother disappeared for a brief time after Bobby was born. Then she returned. If there's precedent, I've reasoned, there must be a pattern. That would only make sense.

So Johnny and I wait together. We stand outside the kitchen and gaze in at the bare cabinets, and the immaculate oven. At the coffee mugs neatly lined up on their racks.

"KHAQQ calling Itasca," I sing to him softly. "We must be on you, but cannot see you."

ACKNOWLEDGEMENTS

My grateful acknowledgement to the editors of the following journals and anthologies in which these stories first appeared, and to the institutions that supported me while this book was taking shape.

Scribner's Best of the Fiction Workshops: "The Retrofit"; Harcourt's Best New American Voices: "Villa of the Veiled Lady"; The Greensboro Review: "The Religious"; The Chicago Review: "The Search for Anna Boubouli"; The Alaska Quarterly Review: "Sweetbreads"; Pennsylvania English: "Letters from H."; 13th Moon: "Parcel Post"; Parakeet: "The Smallest Apartment"; The Cincinnati Review: "Where Nööne is Now"; The Mammoth Anthology of Miniscule Fiction: "I Cook Every Chance."

My gratitude to the New York Foundation for the Arts, Fundación Valparaiso, Brown University, SUNY Albany, Eastern Michigan University, Carnegie Mellon University Press and the Dunham Literary Agency for their generous support.

Carnegie Mellon University Press
Series in Short Fiction

Fortune Telling
David Lynn

A New and Glorious Life
Michelle Herman

The Long and Short of It
Pamela Painter

The Secret Names of Women
Lynne Barrett

The Law of Return
Maxine Rodburg

The Drowning and Other Stories
Edward Delaney

My One and Only Bomb Shelter
John Smolens

Very Much Like Desire
Diane Lefer

A Chapter From Her Upbringing
Ivy Goodman

Happy or Otherwise
Diana Joseph